# Monstrous Crows

**John Brazier**

Matador
Unit E2 Airfield Business Park,
Harrison Road, Market Harborough,
Leicestershire. LE16 7UL
Tel: 0116 2792299
Email: books@troubador.co.uk
Web: www.troubador.co.uk/matador
Twitter: @matadorbooks

ISBN 978 1805142 393

British Library Cataloguing in Publication Data.
A catalogue record for this book is available from the British Library.

Printed and bound in Great Britain by 4edge Limited
Typeset in 11pt Minion Pro by Troubador Publishing Ltd, Leicester, UK

Matador is an imprint of Troubador Publishing Ltd

*For Richard,*
*a brother unlike any of the characters*
*depicted in this novel*

*Special thanks to Neil, Alex, Colin, Melanie,*
*Alison and Michael*

*Tweedledum and Tweedledee*
*Agreed to have a battle;*
*For Tweedledum said Tweedledee*
*Had spoiled his nice new rattle.*

*Just then flew down a monstrous crow*
*As black as a tar-barrel;*
*Which frightened both the heroes so,*
*They quite forgot their quarrel.*

**From** Alice Through the Looking Glass
**by Lewis Carroll**

# Prologue

## May 2010

Urine, sweat and stale cigarette smoke, unconcealed by the reek of cheap disinfectant. Those were the pungent, ubiquitous odours of the caged human male, Mike had long ago decided. It wasn't just the smell of the place that he'd never got used to, it was the dislocated, unexplained sounds of the prison too. The distant shouts, the metallic echoes and then, somehow even worse, the sudden falling of a heavy silence.

The great steel door was swung open and he glanced up at a silent prison officer as he was allowed to pass through the doorway.

'It's not going to be easy, but I need to get out of here as soon as I can,' he thought. 'I shouldn't be here at all. It's all down to big brother in the end.'

It was visiting day, so Mike knew he was going to have to face Andy again. All that self-righteous judgmentalism

– he despised it, but he realised he had little choice. Deep down he was sure he'd done nothing really wrong. The problem had been Andy, because Andy would never understand the way the world works. Whatever's happened with me, he thought, I know he's still analogue in a digital world.

# 1

## June 1979

'It should be illegal!'

Andy looked up from his book. An old man sitting opposite him on the bus was brandishing the local paper.

'What should?' asked the woman sitting next to him, hands clasped in lap, shopping bag at her feet.

'This!' said the man, stabbing his forefinger at a front-page story of personal and family tragedy. 'There should be a law against it. There used to be, until they scrapped it.'

'A law against what?' Her quiet air of resignation suggested to Andy that she must be his wife.

'Suicide! It used to be illegal. Then they changed the law, all those do-gooders. It needs a deterrent. A proper sentence. That would stop it.'

'What sort of a deterrent?'

'Capital punishment. They should bring back the death penalty. That's what.'

1

Andy returned to his book and tried to allow the rattling and wheezing of the bus to drown out the conversation.

He stepped off the bus in the village, swung his school bag over his shoulder and started to walk home up the lane. There was a steady breeze and cumulus scudded through a luminous blue sky above him. He felt a strong urge to leap and punch his fist in the air as he passed the pair of farm cottages before the disused, overgrown railway bridge, or even to hurl himself into the grassy banks beside the lane and roll around in the late-blooming Alexanders.

It would have been a way of celebrating the end of his O-level exams, but Andy had never allowed himself spontaneous celebration. Five long years at the grammar school had seen him develop from a somewhat immature eleven-year-old boy into a serious, rather studious young man. He sometimes wondered why so many families found it important to have a 'clever one'. It wasn't just the negative effect on those deemed less gifted, but the weight of familial responsibility placed upon the shoulders of the chosen.

Andy had found himself in a singular situation throughout his childhood. At primary school most of the other children were from miners' or farmworkers' families and young Andrew was clearly different. His father was a manager at the pit and that meant he had to tread a careful path around some of the boys from families who worked the mines.

He was one of the very few from his school to pass the eleven-plus examination and at grammar school he found himself in a wholly different predicament. Here were the sons of the farmers, the doctors, the solicitors and other white-collar workers. Having a father who worked at the mine, whether as a manager or not, ensured that his status was low and Andy had to fight his corner in the classroom and on the playing fields.

Kent was still a predominantly rural county, even if not quite the Garden of England of years gone by. The digging of coal mines and the arrival of miners, displaced from their local pits around Britain during the early part of the 20th century, had been a shock.

The way the local population had dealt with this was the way in which the English so often deal with things they don't like or don't understand. They pretended it didn't exist, until they came face to face with it and at that point things sometimes turned ugly. Local newspapers posted advertisements for accommodation which baldly stipulated 'no dogs or miners'. Saturday nights in Deal and some of the surrounding villages could become rough when miners and other groups of young men each had enough beer inside them.

Across the fields Andy's family home now came into view, with its traditionally-hung Kentish peg tiles beneath a red roof. It was modest, but it was more pleasing than some of the purely functional building that had taken place in the village to house mine and farm workers before and after the war.

He hung up his schoolbag in the tiny, enclosed porch and went through to the kitchen, where his mother was ironing pants. She looked up, briefly, from where his father's underwear lay steaming on the ironing board.

'Hello Andrew. You're home early.'

'Just had my last exam.'

'Oh, I see. That's nice. Well I'll just finish ironing your father's underwear and then I'll start to make the tea for when your brother comes home.'

Andy had grown used to his mother's growing complacency about his education.

'Mum…'

She looked up again.

'Why do you iron Dad's pants?'

Dorothy Gibbons stopped, set down her iron and looked at her son.

'It's like what your Grandma always said to us when we were little: what if he were to be run over by a bus and didn't have clean, pressed pants on?'

'But Dad drives to work – in the Morris Marina, door to door.'

'Well…' She pondered the issue for a moment. 'He might have to get out for some reason on route.'

'His drive to the pit's cross-country though. There's not a single bus route that way.'

'That's not the point, Andrew. Go and wash your hands and I'll start making tea. Michael will be home shortly.'

The rationale which lay behind the ironing of pants was symptomatic of one of the main contentions which Andy had with his mother. The problem was that she was prepared simply to accept all sorts of pre-digested wisdom, not least of the type she read in her *Daily Express*. While it is a common human failing to jump to a conclusion and then try to find or concoct evidence to support that conclusion, Andy's mother didn't even bother to go that far. The superstructure of her prejudices was completely unsupported by any form of rational substructure.

Andy's father, Ken, accepted his role in life and seemed content to plough the furrow he had been allotted. In contrast, Andy's mother's attitude was best illustrated by the apparently simple question of his place of birth. He was actually born in the nearby cottage hospital, a utilitarian, not to say spartan 19th century institution, where the local miners' and farmworkers' children were all delivered. If asked, however, Dorothy would say that 'Andrew was born in Canterbury', with the implication left hanging in the air that the archbishop might just have conducted his christening.

Andy went upstairs to his room. The door to his younger brother's bedroom was wide open as he passed and there were clothes strewn across the floor as usual. On the wall was a giant Rock Against Racism poster and in an hour or so The Clash would no doubt be pumping out of the stereo system and across the open fields. Mick – as he called himself these days – would tell anyone he wanted to impress that he had been to see the Clash, along with Tom Robinson, Stiff Little Fingers and the rest, at the all-day Rock Against Racism concert in Victoria Park in east London the previous year.

The truth was that the last time he had visited London was some years earlier, along with the rest of the family, to go to the Planetarium and Madame Tussauds. Somehow none of that mattered, because when Mike charmed people with his winning smile truth became a purely subjective matter, a trivial detail.

Andy had often felt close to his little brother as they were growing up, but it seemed that for Mike the real course of their lives was too banal and so he had developed an alternative, parallel narrative that more closely mirrored his ever-changing aspirations.

As he looked out of his bedroom window Andy could see a single bird wheeling and swooping above the corn field. Then down the lane towards the village, he identified the slim, artfully dishevelled figure of his brother, half-walking, half-dancing in the road up to the house, his dark hair in a sort of home-made spiked style, which he had probably contrived at the end of the school day. Along with the slight sense of contempt Andy felt for his little brother's pretentiousness, there was also a sneaking admiration. Mike, it seemed, had a genetic inheritance which Andy somehow lacked.

# 2

## July 1979

'We're one short Sunday,' his older cousin, Jack, had told him. 'Want a game, Andy?'

'Alright.'

'Be down the Welfare field at 1.30.'

'You're playing though?'

'Can't. Got some of the Yorkshire lot coming down. You know, other side of the family.'

Jack's grandfather had been a union convenor in the South Yorkshire coalfield, but he and his family had been forcibly relocated after the industrial unrest at the end of the 1920s.

'I could do without it, Andy, to be honest. They always spend the whole time going on and on about how great Yorkshire is, but I've got to be there and that's that.'

'OK.'

Andy didn't back out, but he wished Jack was going

to be in the team. He'd not been asked to play before and he barely knew, even by sight, any of the other members of the Miners' Welfare Club cricket team. Andy had made a few runs for his school cricket side, but he didn't know how he would manage, playing in a men's team.

Sunday was hot. It had been a mixed summer and there had certainly been none of the parched conditions of 1976 which had left cricket pitches brown, dusty and cracked. Andy could feel a bead of sweat dribble down his temple as he made his way up to the whitewashed breezeblock building behind the cricket pitch.

To call this windowless, flat-roofed cube a pavilion would have been an unsustainable exaggeration. The square and the outfield appeared to be freshly mown, the weather was fine and it might have made an archetypically idyllic English cricketing scene were it not for the very obvious absence of the wealth necessary to maintain the illusion.

Andy carried his bag across the echoing concrete floor of the interior and into the home dressing room. Barely anyone even looked up. Some sort of conversation appeared to be going on among the young men sitting round the perimeter of the room on a low bench. It consisted almost entirely of derivatives of the word 'fuck'. It was a word with which Andy was, of course, familiar, but he had heard it used mainly as a noun or verb, less often as an adjective or adverb and never as a conjunction, preposition or pronoun. Here, the usual rules of grammar did not apply. Andy felt no moral objection, but he did wonder if it wasn't like composing a piece of music in which only a single note could ever be played.

One member of the team was lying rather than sitting on the bench and his face displayed a pallor that suggested he hadn't fully recovered from significant beer intake on Saturday night. Suddenly, he let out a loud, prolonged and potent fart, which enabled all the others to direct their preferred word directly at him.

Finally, one of the members of the team looked up at Andy standing in the doorway. He recognised him as Billy Robson, whose younger brother had been in the same year as Andy at primary school.

'You Andy Gibbons?'

'Yes.'

'Can you bat?'

Andy hesitated. He didn't really bowl and his batting was unspectacular, but it had been good enough for the school under-16s. He had to do something, so he said 'Yes'.

'Go in number six. I won the toss, so we're batting.'

Once the game had started Andy sat a little distance from most of his team-mates, who were smoking roll-ups while sprawled on the grass outside the boundary, a white line hastily – and in places carelessly – painted in the grass. The team's opening batsman was short and muscular and seemed determined to send the fielders as far into the adjacent undergrowth in search of the ball as he possibly could.

When he was out, two short of his fifty, Billy went in and gave the bowlers the same sort of treatment. By the time Andy walked uneasily to the crease the score was 163 for 4.

'Breathe steadily, focus on the ball and move your feet,' he told himself, as if it was a mantra. The bowler, a broad-shouldered man in his early twenties pounded in to the wicket. 'Breathe steadily, focus on the ball and move your feet...' but he barely saw the ball as it went by him, just heard the thud as it landed in the wicket keeper's gloves.

'Nice one Benno. More of that and this little rabbit will be on his way back into the hutch,' shouted the keeper.

Benno ran in again and dug one in a little shorter and a little quicker. Instinctively Andy brought the bat up to protect his face, the ball clipped the bat's shoulder, zipped over the keeper and slip cordon and raced away to the boundary for four.

Andy heard himself breathing hard, as if he was wearing a diver's aqualung. It was the end of the over and he felt only a sense of relief at his own survival.

His innings continued in much the same vein, with not a single run scored in front of the wicket, though as he grew in confidence he started to play some pleasant shots, including a nice late cut down to the boundary between third man and point. Eventually he fell, caught behind, for a respectable nineteen.

One or two of his team-mates glanced up at Andy as he made his way over the boundary and there were a couple of approving nods in his direction. These were difficult men to impress.

During the visiting team's innings Andy ran around in the field, made a few useful stops in the deep and eventually the Welfare team won comfortably enough, by 47 runs.

Later, he packed up his cricket bag in the changing room and headed for the door.

'Alright for next Sunday young 'un?' It was Billy.

'Yes. If you want.'

'We're playing over at Betteshanger. Be at the Bell for one o'clock.'

Andy wandered down the tarmac path in the descending dusk. He noticed a sandy haired figure in the distance, coming towards him. It was a girl, about the same age as him, walking some sort of dog on a lead. As she got closer Andy saw she was wearing a pair of high-waisted jeans and a white t-shirt featuring a faded picture of David Essex. Andy had seen her around the village before, but she didn't go to the grammar school and he didn't know her name. They briefly exchanged eye contact as she passed him.

'Saw you battin' this afternoon.'

Andy turned round. The girl was talking to him.

'Yes.'

'You made some runs.'

'19.'

'Not bad. Some of them bowlers were fast.'

'Yes. Thanks.'

Andy noticed she was looking at him curiously, in a way that people normally didn't. It wasn't uncomfortable, in fact he thought he quite liked it.

'You're Andy Gibbons, aren't you? I know your brother,' said the girl. 'He's two years below me.'

'You're at the high school?'

'That's it. He's a laugh, that one.'

There was a slight catch in her voice, a hint of the rasp which older teenage girls from the village often developed, a tribute to underage smoking, perhaps. Andy had always quite liked this huskiness, which was so different from the trilling sopranos of the grammar school girls.

'I suppose so. What's your name?'

'Susan Cherry. I live over on the estate, up behind the allotments.'

There was a silence, but Andy didn't want to let her go just yet.

'Er…what type of dog is that?'

Susan shrugged. 'Some sort of terrier. Bit of every dog in the neighbourhood, I reckon. My dad just calls it rabbit killer.'

Andy had run out of conversation and he didn't know anything about rabbiting.

'Alright, see you then.'

He turned to go.

'You can kiss me if you want.' She looked at him, calmly and directly in the eyes.

Then she took him by the hand and led him beneath a rather miserable sycamore tree, a little way from the path. She kissed him hard on the mouth. It was an uncompromising, purposeful kiss. When it was over she held his gaze.

'I like you,' she said.

'Well yes, I like you too,' said Andy, a little out of his depth.

'D'you fancy going for a walk? Along the old railway track. We'll have to take the rabbit killer.'

Andy thought about his mum who was expecting him home and would now be preparing his tea.

'Yeah, OK.'

# 3

## August 1979

Andy and Susan wandered through a sun-dappled lane at the edge of the village, past the disused windmill, from which the sails had long since been removed. Just as they had on the first day that they met, they scrambled down the bank towards the old railway line, Andy now clutching the bottle of Woodpecker cider he had persuaded his cousin Jack to buy from the village shop.

They walked through the grasses which grew among the remaining stones and clinkers, where the sleepers and rails had once laid. Here and there wildflowers grew in the rough earth at the edge of the track. Andy found himself reciting the names of the ones he recognised. Susan smiled at him in that shy but knowing way of hers. She was in almost every way just a teenager, but sometimes seemed old beyond her years.

'How do you know all their names?'

'I don't know them all, but the ones I do know, I think I learned in primary school. Mrs Osborne used to take us on what she called nature walks.'

Susan found Andy's free hand and slipped her fingers between his.

After a couple of miles they came to the remains of a railwayman's lineside hut. It was the only building visible for miles around on the low downland, which rolled away into arable fields and woods. The door of the hut was missing and they squeezed inside and sat together in a shaft of sunlight.

The bottle of cider hissed loudly as Andy unscrewed it and a little dribbled down the side before he could screw it tight again. He tried once more, patiently taking the excess carbon dioxide out of it and then passed the bottle to Susan. She drank from it with what seemed like practised ease and passed it back to Andy.

The warmth of the sun and of their bodies pressed close to one another, shoulder to shoulder and thigh to thigh, felt heady, blissful.

'Do you know *Cider with Rosie*?' he asked.

'What, you mix them? Cider and wine?'

He laughed. 'Not rosé – Rosie! It's a book called *Cider with Rosie*. We had to do it for O-level English, but it's really good.'

'Sometimes, I don't know what you're talkin' about Andy…but don't stop, I like it.'

'Well it's by a man called Laurie Lee and he wrote poems too. There's a good one about coming back to Kent after being abroad. I really like the last verse:

*'So do I breathe the hayblown airs of home,*
*And watch the sea-green elms drip birds and shadows,*
*And as the twilight nets the plunging sun,*
*My heart's keel slides to rest among the meadows.'*

'I like the way it sounds, but I don't know what it means.'

'It means he's happy to be home. It's just a different way of saying it. And that last line says how I feel now, much better than I ever could. When I'm with you, well… my heart's keel slides to rest,' he said, a little bashfully.

Susan rested her head on Andy's shoulder and they sat in the sun, cocooned in their own little world.

They barely noticed the colour fade gently from the sky and the slow fall of night. Venus rose just above the horizon and their world grew velvet black, yet it never occurred to either of them to go back to their homes.

Susan turned to Andy, gently pulled his face towards hers and kissed him with a passion and intensity he had never experienced before. Unlike Andy, Susan was neither ambiguous nor ambivalent and that kiss expressed simple desire.

When he looked back on it, Andy felt that what happened next he remembered less like a film than as a series of powerful, enduring still images – mental photographs – imprinted forever on his memory. He was equally able to recall exactly the feel of her body and the smell of her hair. First experiences are rarely the best. There is often too much self-consciousness, too much sexual tension, but Susan showed no inhibitions. She may have been young, but she was a passionate and considerate lover and the events of that evening, in the silent darkness of the Kent countryside, sealed their relationship in a way that felt indelible to Andy.

Afterwards they lay together in their hut for an hour or more. Hardly a word was spoken and for perhaps the first time in his life Andy felt no words were necessary. Eventually they crawled back out through the doorway and into the night. Venus had gone, but now the moon was rising and the three mile walk back to the village seemed all too short to Andy.

They stood briefly outside Susan's house, which was typical of the low-cost housing thrown up to provide cheap accommodation for miners' families in the interwar years. They kissed farewell and it was a kiss that Andy wished would never end.

'Susan, I...'

'Don't say nothing,' she said, with that faint rasp in her voice. 'You don't need to and it's best not.' She turned and walked down the path to her front door, her slight frame casting a shadow in the moonlight.

# 4

## June 1980

Andy was at the tiny table in his room which he used as a desk. He was half-way through an essay, but he was thinking about Susan, something he found himself doing more and more, when he wasn't thinking about John Donne or William Ewart Gladstone.

So much of his life was bound up with school work now. He wanted to get the A-level grades he needed for university and sometimes he even enjoyed the courses he was studying. Inevitably though, that meant there was less time in which to see Susan. For her part, she would disappear from his life for days, even weeks on end and then suddenly re-appear like a southerly gale, disruptive yet irresistible and infused with warmth.

Andy disliked these periods apart, but didn't like to phone her. Susan's father was a man of few words and his abrupt telephone manner was not untypical of an ex-

17

miner who had subsequently gone to work on the ferries out of Dover. By all accounts both jobs required him to anaesthetise himself with alcohol most evenings. He was often the last man standing in the Bell and sometimes he couldn't even manage that.

Andy hadn't seen Susan for almost a fortnight, but that Friday afternoon she had suddenly appeared as he stepped off the bus on the way back from school. She had slipped her arm into his, given him that smile which she knew he couldn't resist and said she'd meet him at the bus stop at six. It was not their usual rendezvous. Neither of them had much money and as a result they were usually confined to walking around the village, or in the surrounding countryside.

Now Andy put down his pen, then after he had bathed and changed he walked down to the bus stop in the early evening sunshine. Susan was already there. As he approached he thought – not for the first time – how lovely she looked, certainly much more alluring than Gladstone, who had taken up more than enough of his time that week.

Andy kissed her shyly, almost as if it was the first time, even though they had been – more or less – together for nearly a year.

'D'you know where we're going?' she asked.

'I didn't know we were going anywhere.'

She smiled.

'We're going to Dreamland.'

Andy was taken by surprise. Dreamland was a semi-mythical place, a seafront fairground full of noise and light, with undertones of sexual tension and the smell of candyfloss in the air. Unfortunately it was in distant Margate, the sort of place that the villagers normally visited just once a year and then only on an organised outing. Andy's excitement was soon doused by his sense of realism.

'Sorry Susan, I can't. I've hardly any money.' He held out the few coppers he had in his palm.

Susan fixed him with that gaze of hers, slid her hand down into the pocket of her jeans and retrieved a crumpled £10 note, flourishing it proudly.

'Where did you get that?'

'Don't matter, I got it,' she smiled. 'Bus'll be here in a couple of minutes and we can get the last one back.'

Not for the first time, any misgivings Andy may have had were swept away by this pretty young woman's irresistible enthusiasm and unambiguous sense of purpose.

Margate had been a receptacle for dreams – at least for people from parts of London and Kent – for almost two hundred years. It was here, early in the previous century, that the paddle steamers first put in, having plied the Thames estuary from the capital. On board one of them had been the painter JMW Turner and here he stayed, on and off, for thirty years, declaring to the patron and critic John Ruskin that the place had the loveliest skies in Europe. In reality it may not only have been the sunsets, but also the earthier attractions of his landlady, Mrs Booth, that kept Turner returning to the Isle of Thanet.

Margate's second wave crashed upon the shores of the nation's consciousness in the years after the second world war. A people desperately in need of entertainment and distraction found in Margate what they seemed to lack in everyday life. So, they came in their thousands by train and charabanc, down from London and out from the fields and coal mines of Kent.

By the beginning of the 1980s though, it looked as if a third wave was beyond this resort, as it was beyond many other seaside towns up and down the country. Dreamland was emblematic of that decline. It was threadbare, its glory days were gone, it was the fifty-year-old applying make-up in front of the mirror and imagining still being twenty-one.

Margate had never been a wealthy or stylish resort, but somehow the sense of excitement and novelty, the loud music and flashing lights, meant that that didn't matter. At least it didn't matter all that much until affordable holidays on the costas of Spain lured British working-class holidaymakers away to places where it rarely rained and where the north-easterlies didn't whip in off the North Sea.

That June evening though, was unusually balmy. The lights of the amusement arcades rolled and blinked at them like a giant fruit machine, as Andy and Susan stepped off the bus on Margate seafront and made their way into the fabled grounds of Dreamland. Its heyday may have long gone, but the traces of that era were all too evident. Everything looked as if it could do with a fresh coat of paint and the scuffs and scratches on the rides could easily have been left by the mods and rockers who regularly turned the seafront into a battleground in the early 1960s.

'C'mon, I love this one,' squealed Susan, grabbing Andy's hand and dragging him towards the Waltzer. A grubby teenager took their money and tried to short-change them, but Andy had already calculated what they were owed and the boy looked disappointed to have failed to dupe such apparently soft targets.

As the Waltzer hurled them round and round Susan screamed happily and clung onto Andy, the lights and the speed making their heads spin and giving them no chance to think. When Andy looked back on his life many years later, this was one of the moments when he seemed most at one with the world. Nothing else seemed to matter apart from Susan and the simple sensations they both experienced in that instant. The world may have been pregnant with possibilities, but none of them even seemed to concern him.

That set the tone for the next couple of hours: 'Oh God, I love candyfloss…let's go on the Wild Mouse…win me a cuddly toy!' Andy tried to and he hit three cards with his darts, but the artfully blunted tips ensured they fell out again. He didn't even mind that, because he was happy just being with Susan in this place that was so unlike the rest of his life. Inevitably though, their money ran out, as he knew it would and they had little more than enough for the ride home.

The night bus wove through the dimly lit streets, with Andy and Susan at the front of the top deck. As it rumbled to the top of an incline, a view of the harbour at Ramsgate unfolded before them and an incandescent June moon left a trail of silver across the surface of the water. When the bus reached the West Cliff, Susan impulsively grabbed Andy's hand, pulled him down the stairs and off the bus. Andy stood on the kerbside watching its tail-lights disappear into the night.

'What are you doing? That bus would have taken us all the way home.'

Susan didn't even bother to answer. She was gazing out to sea.

'Just look at that,' was all she said. An ethereal band of moonlight lit the sea all the way from Pegwell Bay to where it lapped the foot of the West Cliff, way below them.

'Come on, let's go to the boating lake.'

'It'll be closed by now.'

'I know, I know. Doesn't matter.'

They walked, laughing, hand in hand along the deserted promenade until they reached the boating lake perched on top of the cliff. The little paddle boats were lined up silently in the reflected moonlight.

'Look! That one's not chained up to the others,' said Susan, turning to Andy with a look of excitement on her face. There was no time for him to issue a warning before she was over the fence and climbing into the little unsecured paddle boat. Laughing, Susan manoeuvred the tiny craft away from the side and towards the centre of the lake. Andy called to her, but she couldn't hear him, because now she was singing.

*I am sailing,*
*I am sailing,*
*Home again,*
*'Cross the sea.'*

'Susan! Come back!' called Andy, but now she had reached the centre of the lake and was rising unsteadily to her feet, the little boat tipping one way and then the other.

She stood in the moonlight, arms away from her sides to steady herself, a little like a twentieth century vision of Aphrodite, with the tiny paddle boat as her scallop shell.

*'I am sailing,*
*Stormy waters,*
*To be near you,*
*To be free...'*

Susan took a step back on to the little craft's bench seat and the boat lurched and then capsized as Susan fell into the water with a shriek.

'I can't swim!' she shouted and that was the last Andy saw of her.

He kicked off his shoes and without thinking ran to the edge and jumped into the freezing water. To his surprise he jarred his knees on the bottom and fell headlong into the lake. When he managed to stand up he realized the water was less than three feet deep. He could see the paddle boat, but there was no sign of Susan, so he strode off through the lake in the darkness.

As he reached the upturned boat he saw Susan in the water beyond it. She squealed with laughter and Andy felt a great surge of relief.

'What were you thinking of, Susan?'

'I knew you'd come! I knew you'd come!' she shouted in delight.

'You said you couldn't swim.'

'I can't, but I can paddle!' She howled with laughter. 'I knew I didn't need to swim and I knew you'd come!'

With that she threw her arms around Andy and gave

him a kiss of such passion and force that he almost fell backwards into the lake. He knew he should feel more disgruntled than he did, but it was hard to be angry with her. There was something about her spontaneity and her undiluted appetite for life that he didn't simply like. He envied it. Susan slipped her hand into his and they waded to the side of the lake together.

Back on dry land they turned to look at one another, soaked and dripping, then burst into laughter. There was nothing else for it, so Andy and Susan squelched back up the hill to the main road.

They sat on the top deck of the bus in exhausted silence. It was Susan, in unusually reflective mood, who eventually spoke.

'Do you want kids, Andy?'

'Not right now, I'm still at school.'

Susan was undeterred.

'If I had children, I wouldn't want to – you know – put pressure on them like your mum and dad have on you.'

'My parents don't really do that. It's me as much as them.'

'I'd just want my kids to be happy. I'd make sure they knew that I didn't mind what they did as long as they were happy.'

'Isn't that a type of pressure?'

'What do you mean?'

'Well, most of us aren't really designed to be happy all the time. Not truly happy.'

'Why's that?'

'Evolution, maybe.'

'What?'

'Well, you know, it's probably just a quirk of evolution. I think I read it somewhere. Too much happiness and contentment takes away the human desire to strive.'

'So?'

'So, what you're saying is just another type of pressure. If your children know your main ambition for them is just that they are happy, they'll probably feel like failures every time they're unhappy.'

'I'd just want my kids to live for the moment like me.'

'I can't live that way. I'd feel frustrated.'

'Why?' She was genuinely amazed.

'Well if you think about it, it's not often that the moment we live in is much better than boring or ordinary and if you're not planning ahead then you've nothing to look forward to either.'

'You think too much, Andy,' she said with a frown, but still snuggled her damp body up against his.

# 5

## September 1981

The sun was sinking in the sky above the fields and woods where Andy and Susan had roamed when they first met.

Andy wheeled his bike out from the old brick wash-house in the garden. His father was harvesting potatoes, digging them up with a fork and dropping them into a battered plastic bucket. Incongruously dressed in an ancient baggy suit, the sort of thing he might have been issued with after his National Service in the East Kent Regiment, he straightened up when he saw Andy and ran a hand through his thinning hair.

'Are you off out?' he asked, rather unnecessarily.

'Yes, I'm going over to the Welfare Club to have a drink with cousin Jack.'

'Bags all packed for college?'

'University.'

'It's the same thing.'

'Yes, I'm all packed, right down to neatly ironed pants and socks.'

'Your mum likes to look after us, you know.'

'She does, she does.'

'What time does your train leave on Saturday morning?'

'9.43'

'Do you want a lift to the station in the Marina?'

'Yes, thanks.'

'Well, give my regards to young Jack,' he said, turning to bury his fork in the chalky soil again.

'He's 21, Dad.'

'All the same. Oh, and if you see your little brother, send him home!'

Andy swung his leg over the crossbar and pedalled his bike out into the lane. As the sun went down the gentle folds of the Kentish countryside slowly revealed winding hedgerows, newly-stubbled golden fields, old chalk quarries and tiny hamlets hidden away in natural hollows.

Then, suddenly and incongruously, the headgear of the pit swung into view. Vast functional interwar brick buildings jostled around the 3,000 feet deep shaft and loomed over the surrounding fields. A substantial piece of the industrial north had, it seemed, been ripped from its roots and parachuted into the Garden of England.

As he cycled past the main gates Andy noticed a clutch of crudely flyposted red and yellow handbills advising people to vote for Tony Benn in the Labour Party's imminent deputy leadership election. Kent was still a militant coalfield. Many of the miners' families had originally been sent to the county as a result of their involvement in industrial action and their consequent reputations for union activism acquired in other parts of the country. This was potentially fertile ground for the Benn campaign.

Andy parked his bike outside the Miners' Welfare Club, a purely functional blockhouse which had been designed to rigorously exclude any aesthetic features whatsoever. A familiar figure was engaged in flyposting bills to the exterior of the club. His dark hair was more ragged and less punk-inspired than it had been and he now had the beginnings of a first beard.

'What are you doing, Mike?'

Mike turned. 'It's Mick. You should know that by now. What do you think I'm doing?'

'OK. Why are you doing it then?'

'Direct action. We've got to take control of the situation. Got to get Tony Benn elected. I went into Canterbury and flyposted the Cathedral last night,' Mike added with a touch of pride.

'Well that should have sown up the ecclesiastical vote.'

'Not funny. It's not the point either, I'm sticking it to the man.'

'Which man?'

'You know, the establishment, the upper classes, the aristos, the toffs and all the state apparatus that protects them.'

'Well good luck with that. I imagine you think you know what you're doing. I'm going in to have a farewell pint or two with Jack.'

'I'll come with you.'

'Finished sticking it to the man then? Dad wants you to go home by the way and you realise they'll not serve you alcohol in here, even with that growth on your chin. Most people know you're my little brother.'

The interior of the club was as utilitarian as it was outside, but the beer was cheap and there were some good sessions, especially on a Friday or Saturday night, when the bar was loud and a miasma of tobacco smoke hung in the air. Not many of the – largely male – drinkers would come up and talk to Andy though. This wasn't the result of any particular animosity, but because they knew he was different. He was connected to management.

Jack got the beers in, along with a Britvic orange for Andy's brother.

'There you go, Mike.'

'Mick!' said Mike, who looked sulkily at his juice and then went off to flypost the toilets.

'Well then Mastermind, are you looking forward to it?' asked Jack.

Jack was a junior electrician at the pit. Wiry and athletic with a sardonic wit, he was not just Andy's cousin, but his friend and confidant.

'I suppose so. I just don't know what it'll be like. You know. It's outside my experience. Will it be a bit like school? Will the others be like the ones off University Challenge? Will I have to talk like them? I don't know.'

'From what I understand, there's a lot of serious shagging to be done.'

'Well, I'm still going out with Susan you know. At least I think I am. I'll see her in the vacations anyway.'

Mike came back, looking guilty and triumphant.

After a while one of the faces at the bar turned towards them in recognition. Kenny Roberts must have been about the same age as Jack, because they'd been to school together before Kenny had gone to work down the pit at sixteen. Andy vaguely knew him from the local cricket league. Kenny came over to where they were sitting. It was clear he had been in the club for some time, probably since his shift had finished.

'Alright Jack, mate,' said Kenny. 'How's it going?'

'Not bad.'

'He's a great laugh, old Jack,' said Kenny to Andy. 'So quick. We was up in Blackpool a few years back and he give the funniest comeback I ever heard. Gonna get another drink in, then I'll tell you about it.' Kenny wove his way unsteadily back to the bar.

'When did you go to Blackpool with Kenny?' asked Andy.

'I've never been there with him. In fact, I've never been there at all. He says this just about every time he sees me, but it wasn't me.'

'Seriously? Why not put him right?'

'Well at first I was flattered. You know. I guess that over twenty years or so you get knocked back for things you never did, but it's not often you get people patting you on the back for stuff you didn't do. I suppose I just thought it was payback time.'

'So what's the story then?'

'I don't know, I can never bring myself to listen to it, knowing it wasn't me, because I wasn't even there.'

Kenny returned with his pint.

'Was you up here Saturday night?' he asked.

They all shook their heads.

'Shoulda' been. Eddie Sutcliffe gave Dave Goodwin a right hammering out back. Both really pissed up.'

'What was it about?' asked Andy.

'No idea.' Kenny looked unconcerned that there was apparently no motive for the fight. 'It got broke up in the end. It's just what lads do on a Saturday night, isn't it?'

There was a silence, except for the clink of glasses and hum of conversation in the club.

'Anyway boys,' said Kenny, brightening, 'I was telling you about Jack here. We was walking past the Tower Ballroom in Blackpool and these two girls come up to us. And one of them says to Jack…' Kenny sniggered.

'Sorry, just need a slash,' said Jack, rising quickly to his feet and disappearing.

Kenny was undeterred and continued with lager-fuelled enthusiasm.

By the time Jack returned, the story was complete and Andy and Mike glanced at Jack with a sort of quizzical admiration, in spite of his earlier disclaimers.

'Anyway,' said Kenny, now in full flow, 'Did you hear the one about Joe Gormley?' He didn't wait for a response.

'So Gormley dies and he goes to heaven and St Peter tells him he can come in. "Hang on," says Gormley, "I'm not setting foot inside those pearly gates if Arthur Scargill's coming here." Gormley hates Scargill. So Peter says, "No, no, Scargill's going to the other place down below, if you know what I mean." Anyway, some years later Gormley goes up to St Peter and says, "I've got a bone to pick with you. You said Scargill wasn't coming to heaven, but I saw him yesterday, driving around in that big Jag of his. Only

Scargill drives a Jag like that." St Peter just smiled and said, "No, you're mistaken. That wasn't him, it was God. He just thinks he's Arthur Scargill!"'

Kenny laughed long and loud at his own joke, rose unsteadily to his feet and was about to return to the bar, his mission accomplished.

'Wait!' said Mike, who had remained silent throughout the earlier exchanges. He rummaged in his bag and removed a flier – *Vote Tony Benn for Deputy Leader* – which he gave to Kenny. He in turn stared at it for a bit, gave Mike a look of incomprehension and dropped the handbill lightly back on the table, before weaving his way into the crowd again.

# 6

## June 1982

Andy's first year at university passed in a blur. When he looked back on that time he thought of it as perhaps the greatest influence, the most important catalyst in his life, more significant even than his relationship with Susan, who he still saw from time to time. He had tried writing to her at first, but she never wrote back. Still, when they met in the vacations they seemed, almost miraculously, as much a couple as they ever had been, with all the shared laughter and passion they had had before Andy went away.

Perhaps he was so caught up in his new life and the effect that university had on him, that Andy didn't fully appreciate all the changes which had been taking place elsewhere, not least at home.

In particular, much about his little brother was different. He was, apparently, no longer called Mick, but Mike (which was what Andy had always called him anyway). He was as unemployed as he had been a year earlier, when he left school, but now he was at least making noises about finding a job. How he was going to do this was not made explicit, but his current preference was no longer to be a racing driver, but an estate agent. Or an accountant. Or, if not, a nightclub owner.

Most notable, however, was the 180 degree turn he had affected in his political allegiance. This became clear on one of those long English summer days which seem to go on forever, when the rain lashes down and embeds itself against the window panes. Time was a sluggard that day and Andy and Mike sat confined together in the little front room of their parents' home, watching lunchtime television, socked feet draped across the furniture in a way that their mother would not have approved of.

The familiar figure of the Prime Minister appeared on the screen.

'She's doing a great job, you know,' said Mike, admiringly.

There was a long silence while Andy took this information in.

'Who?'

'Mrs Thatcher.'

'You hate her.'

'No.'

'I remember when you were part of the workers' revolution plotting to overthrow her.'

'No.'

'Oh yes, you were. What was it about getting rid of the toffs and aristos and the apparatus of the state protecting the establishment? What about sticking it to the man?'

'But she's not from the establishment. Don't you see that?'

'Sorry? You're saying the Prime Minister is not part of the establishment?'

'She's…I don't know…a greengrocer's daughter or something. And what about the Falklands?' asked Mike, becoming even more animated.

'Oh yes, that scattering of rocks thousands of miles away in the South Atlantic Ocean.'

'She was pretty magnificent,' said Mike gushingly. 'You've got to admire her balls.'

'Do you want to re-phrase that?'

'You know – her conviction and self-belief, that streak of ruthless single-mindedness in seeing it through.'

'A lot of men died,' said Andy quietly.

'You wait and see. She'll make the difference in this country. Things are going to change.'

Andy shook his head and returned his attention to the screen.

A few minutes later their mother burst in, wordlessly removed their feet from the armrests of the sofa and chairs and started to tidy around them.

'What are you doing?' asked Mike.

'I just need to clean and tidy before Mrs Byrne comes.'

'But she's the cleaner.'

'Don't you pay her to do the cleaning?' asked Andy.

'Yes, I know, but I wouldn't want her to think we don't live in a clean house.'

Andy and Mike looked at one another. Eyebrows were raised and shoulders shrugged. The logic inherent in this was apparently unassailable.

That, as it turned out, was almost the last genuinely fraternal connection between them for some time.

\*

'Fancy yomping down the village for a pint?' asked Mike, that evening.

'Yomping? We're going to the Bell, not taking Mount Tumbledown. Funny how winning a small colonial war makes militarism so popular.'

It had stopped raining and Andy and Mike wandered along the glistening lane, the air fresh with the scents of summer in the damp English countryside.

'Must be three months since I was last in the Bell. Still much the same, I suppose?' asked Andy.

'Yeah, I was in last Saturday with Susan…'

Mike tailed off, aware that he might have said too much.

'Susan who? You've never been out with any Susans.'

Mike said nothing and an unpleasant thought began to dawn on Andy.

'Was it Susan Cherry?'

'Maybe.'

'You've been out with my girlfriend?'

Mike said nothing.

'Have you slept with her?'

'Probably.'

'You can't remember? You "probably" slept with Susan Cherry?'

'Yeah.' Mike did his best to look unconcerned.

There was a silence while Andy took this in.

'You shagged my girlfriend!'

'I thought it was all over now you're at college.'

'University!'

'I didn't know you two were still…you know, whatever you call it…an item.'

'You might have bloody asked.'

'What for? Permission? Please may I screw your girlfriend, big brother?'

'You bastard!'

'Listen Andy, monogamy – it's just a bourgeois convention.'

'A bourgeois convention? You're a Tory now, remember. Bourgeois convention is what being a Tory is all about.'

'Alright, well we might even get married so then it'll all be OK I guess.'

Andy turned and walked back home, alone. Those were the last words the brothers exchanged for fifteen months.

# 7

## August 1984

Time may heal rifts, but it doesn't necessarily change trajectories. Andy and Mike had made peace with one another at Christmas 1983. Life had moved on and Susan Cherry was no longer a part of either of their respective worlds. All the same, not only could the scars be traced, but there were still signs that the healing process was incomplete. This manifested itself in a renewed sibling rivalry of pettiness and pedantry, of attempting to outdo or undermine one another.

One afternoon the following summer Andy and Mike strolled down the widest part of the pedestrianised main street in Canterbury, passing a man selling vehicle breakdown services while standing under a large orange and white umbrella. It wasn't clear why he thought a street full of pedestrians would provide a receptive audience for his wares, but as the brothers approached, he stepped forward.

'Can I interest you in a fully comprehensive breakdown service, gentlemen?'

'No thanks, I'm with the AA,' said Mike. 'Haven't had a drink for years,' he added with a grin.

'Very droll, sir, I've not heard that one before,' the salesman replied without registering any amusement.

'I sometimes wonder just how embarrassing you'd have to be for me to refuse to come out in public with you,' said Andy bitterly, as they strolled on.

The market was coming to an end and the traders were shutting up their stalls.

'Forty pence a punnet,' shouted one of the stallholders, waving a punnet of strawberries. 'That's all I want, for-ty pence a punnet!'

'Watch this,' said Mike and wandered over to the stall.

'I'll give you 25p.'

'For-ty pence a punnet!'

'OK, two for 40p'

'I'm closing up ladies and gents – for-ty pence a punnet!' yelled the man, then under his breath to Mike, 'do us a favour mate and just fuck off.'

'OK, OK 30p then. Final offer.'

'For-ty pence a punnet!'

'That seemed to go well,' said Andy as they wandered on down the street towards the West Gate. 'What were you trying to demonstrate there?'

'Listen, you've got to take every opportunity these days and the way things are going there will be a lot of them, believe me. Never pay the full price, never pay at all unless you have to, never…'

'Give a sucker an even break? That's a lovely philosophy.

What do you imagine would happen if everyone operated like that?'

'But not everybody does, that's the point. Only the enterprising will survive.'

'But how is underpaying – or not paying at all – enterprising? What have you done...' Andy could feel his irritation rising '...what have you created, what have you stimulated, in what way have you done anything worthwhile?'

'Listen Andy, it's all about these market force things, OK? Market forces decide everything in life.'

'Really? Where did you get that notion from?'

'I heard it on the news. It was that...er...you know – Freda Milkman.'

'Who?'

'You know, the economist, Mrs T's guru.'

'You mean Milton Friedman.'

'Something like that. Anyway, the point is that we need to stop busybodies interfering in the market.'

'What?'

'We don't need these government whatsits for a start.'

'What whatsits?'

'You know, these quango things. We don't need financial regulation, we don't need trading standards or health and safety or any of that other stuff.'

He was warming to his theme now, starting to feel confident, having apparently sorted the issue out to his satisfaction in his own head.

'The point is that the market decides everything, OK? If you can sell it and someone wants to buy it, that's fine. Just agree a price and get on with it.'

'Really? Have you thought this through?'

Mike looked nettled, but Andy continued.

'So according to you, it's OK to sell – just off the top of my head – sub-machine guns, junk bonds, class A drugs, child pornography and I don't know…a whole load of other noxious stuff, as long as someone wants to buy it?'

Mike shook his head, as if in sorrow at his brother's obtuseness, but Andy hadn't finished. It was his turn to feel irritated and he adopted the didactic attitude that he knew infuriated his little brother.

'One of the problems, Mike, is that it's all so alluring, isn't it? With most economists, after hearing them explain their theories you tend to think you know less than you did when they started speaking. But with these people who call themselves monetarists it's all deceptively straightforward. The market is God. That's it. People like the theory because it's so simple that anyone can understand it. That doesn't mean that it's right though.'

'You don't get it yet Andy, but you will. You will. Wait and see what I've got back at the parents' house. Then you'll see the direction I'm headed in.'

*

Andy sat at the table in the little kitchen, gazing out over the field of ripening corn blowing gently in the wind, as it stretched away towards a disused quarry. His mind was pleasantly in neutral until Mike bounced in with a brown cardboard box under his arm.

'What've you got there?'

'What I have here is something that will be in

every home in the country within three years. This is a prototype, but once production is underway it's going to be a knockout, an overnight success, a…'

'You're setting up a manufacturing operation?'

Mike looked shocked.

'Manufacturing is dead in this country, Andy. Labour is too expensive and too unreliable. Selling is what it's all about. It's where the big money is.'

'So how do you come by whatever this is?'

'We are going to have it made where wages are minimal and health and safety is unheard of.'

'Globally, that doesn't really narrow it down much.'

'Malaysia. No, I mean Indonesia. Or maybe it's Micronesia.'

'Milk of Magnesia?'

Mike gave Andy a withering look. He clearly wanted this to be taken very seriously.

'OK, so what exactly is this product which every home will have?'

Theatrically, Mike withdrew a plastic cube from the cardboard and placed it on the kitchen table.

'A plastic box. I think most homes have these already.'

'No, no, no,' said Mike, as if desperate to maintain his own enthusiasm.

'It's a defroster,' he added with some pride.

'A defroster? How does it work?'

'Well first you plug it in.' Mike produced an electric cable from the back of the box and plugged it in to a socket with a flourish. A small dial lit up on the front of the box.

'You take whatever you want from your freezer, place it in the defroster, set the dial to the time you began the process and then take the food out again once the defrosting time stated on the packet is up.'

'How does the dial control the defrosting?'

'It's manual, you set it by hand.'

'It's not a clock then?'

'No. This way you have full manual control.'

'You mean it doesn't do anything.'

'It shows when you took the frozen food out of the freezer, so you know when it's defrosted.'

'As long as you set it and then look at your watch. And it contains no heating device to accelerate the defrosting process?'

'That's the beauty of it, it's an entirely natural product.'

'Except for the plastic and the little light which illuminates the dial.'

'I'll be a millionaire before I'm twenty-five.'

'You'll be prosecuted by Trading Standards long before then. Just so I'm clear, your wonder product which is going to take the market by storm is, in fact, a plastic box with a small low wattage bulb and a dial which doesn't function independently?'

'The growth of home freezers in this country has been massive over recent years. They're all going to need a defroster.'

'Really? And what's the retail price going to be?'

'£29.99'

'£29.99!'

'£49.99 for two.'

'Fifty quid for two plastic boxes. People would have to have lost their senses to pay that.'

'Yeah, that's what I'm counting on.'

# 8

## February 1985

In the pale sun of a morning that offered a hint of Spring, Andy stood astride the old Vespa he had recently bought, gazing across the field at a bird of prey wheeling high above it.

He was also looking out for a figure walking along the lane. However, the one trudging towards him was not the one he was hoping to see.

Mike was making his way up to the house.

'Andy!' he started, as if he hadn't seen and recognised his brother from 150 yards away. 'What are you looking at?'

'You see that bird hovering over the field there?'

'It's just a gull or a crow,' said Mike.

Andy was unable to conceal his look of disdain.

'I think it might be a red kite. They're really rare. They were once thought to be extinct in this country.'

'So what are you doing out here, nature boy?'

'Just waiting for Jack. We're going up the club.'

'I don't know why you still go there,' Mike retorted. 'Bunch of losers. You realise those miners tried to hold the country to ransom with their strike. All they're interested in is money – more and more and more money.'

'I think you'll find the strike was about pit closures. They're afraid of losing their jobs. It might suit Thatcher and Scargill to make out that it's about radical politics, but for most of the men and their families it's about survival. What do you imagine the career options are for the average unemployed miner round here?'

Mike showed his contempt for the question.

'Who cares? They're the enemy within. We don't need those people. They're history and history is just about what's dead and buried. The union has lost, but they won't admit it, because they're so stubborn and this lot, the Kent miners, are the worst. I'm sure they'll be the last to go back to work. I bet they'd even picket Scargill if he told them to go back!'

'Sometimes our strengths are also our weaknesses, Mike.'

'What?'

'What I mean is, loyalty is a great quality, but in the wrong circumstances it can develop into a self-destructive stubbornness.'

'Oh really?'

'Yes, just like a plant growing in the wrong place is a weed.'

'Grasshopper.'

'What?'

'Andy, you must remember that TV programme with

45

David Carradine – Kung Fu! All fake eastern wisdom.'

'Thanks.'

*

A few minutes later, Jack strolled along the lane and climbed onto the back of the Vespa, which Andy kick-started angrily, still irritated by the conversation with his brother. They headed for the Welfare Club.

At the junction at the bottom of the lane, on the edge of the village, Andy brought the scooter to a halt as a dirty white bus came into view. As it approached, he and Jack could see the tell-tale metal grilles affixed to the windows. The bus drew up just beyond the junction and the door opened. A few men climbed off, looked up and down the empty street and slunk, in silence, away to their homes.

Andy and Jack knew what this was – the scabs' bus. Andy watched them go and recognised a number of faces. Most were miners with young families. They were men with bills to pay and mouths to feed. They each knew that in terms of the life of the village and the pit, they were finished. Whatever had compelled them to return to work and cross the picket lines, they would now pay a heavy price.

It wouldn't be long before they found out exactly how great that price was to be, because the strike was coming to an end. In as much as the miners could be said to have won the strikes of the 1970s, they had all but lost this one. Andy couldn't help feeling that it was not just the losing combatants who would suffer the consequences of defeat, but their families and their entire communities.

As swiftly as it had arrived, the bus slipped away up the empty village street and out of sight. Silence returned, save for the sound of Andy's Vespa pulling away in the direction of the club.

*

The club was nearly deserted, with just one or two desultory drinkers nursing lonely pints.

'I haven't seen much of your little brother recently, Andy,' said Jack.

'No. He wouldn't come up here now. He seems to have undergone some sort of personality transplant.'

'What?'

'He's completely fixated on some sort of yuppie dream. All he knows is that he's going to be rich and he doesn't care how he gets there.'

'It's death or glory for him then.'

'In as much as he'll either end up a millionaire or a criminal. Or possibly both.'

'And how's that job of yours going? It is a proper job you've got, isn't it?' asked Jack, still a little in awe of his educated cousin, but reluctant to reveal it.

'Yes, it's not a government scheme or part of the Youth Opportunities Programme.'

'Are you going to be an award-winning reporter then? Any big scoops?'

'It's just the local paper and I've only been there three months. This week I'm writing about a lecture to the local Women's Institute on the subject of macramé, an amateur dramatic production of Noel Coward's *Hay Fever* and a primary school Easter Bonnet Parade. I'm not convinced I'll get a Pulitzer Prize for any of those pieces. It's alright for a first job though. In fact I'm enjoying it. I'm not paid much, but it's a start. What about you, Jack?'

'Not great at the moment, is it? Once the miners have gone back we'll see what happens with the pits. But I've no great hopes for the Kent ones. Apart from Betteshanger they're not producing anything much at all and the government knows there are still plenty of militants down here so they'll want to make an example of them, I guess.'

'That doesn't mean the pits will just close down though.'

'You've got to remember that this strike was personal – on both sides. Scargill hates the Tory government, thinks he's at the cutting edge of a workers' revolution and Thatcher hates the miners because of what they did to the Tories in the '70s. Either way, if there's no pit then there's no need for electricians working in the pit.'

'At least you've got skills you can use in another industry.'

'Maybe. Won't pay much though, will it? I'll tell you what it feels like. You remember when we all used to go down to Deal and muck around on the beach?'

'Of course.'

'Sometimes we'd stand right by the water's edge and if there was a bit of a swell on and – especially if there was an ebb tide – when a wave broke and then went back out again you couldn't stand up. The stones beneath your feet used to move and the seawater would grab you by the ankles and try to drag you in. That's what it feels like at the moment, living round here…oh listen, I'm just a bit down today, Andy. You get off if you want to. I've got to hang around in the club. I'm waiting for Albert Ormondroyd.'

'Who?'

'My great-uncle, on my mum's side of the family. The ones who stayed in Yorkshire. Uncle Albert retired from the pit last year and now he's doing a sort of farewell tour of his relations.'

'He worked in the South Yorks coalfield?'

'Started when he was fifteen. Finished up at Christmas. Down the pits all his working life. He was at Lofthouse when they had the disaster there in '73. Never met him, but he's a real old Yorkshire pitman apparently.'

'I might hang on and have a word with him, if that's alright. Maybe there's a story there. You know, something a bit different from all the bad stuff around mining at the moment.'

'Alright, Mum's bringing him up when she starts her shift behind the bar. I want to slip away and place a bet, so it'd be good if you could keep him entertained for me.'

'What time will Auntie Sheila be bringing him up?'

'About one.'

*

Albert Ormondroyd was a small, grizzled man, the topography of his face, with its steep escarpments and deep, lined gullies, seeming to speak of decades of hard labour down the pit. Outside it had turned into an unseasonably warm afternoon, but in the club Ormondroyd still wore his thick gaberdine coat, topped off by a flat cap and muffler.

'Can I buy you a pint Mr Ormondroyd?' asked Andy.

'Aye lad.'

Auntie Sheila poured two pints and smiled as she looked up at Andy.

'Good luck with him, love. I'm not sure you'll get much out of him.'

'I'll do my best. It'll be good practice,' said Andy as he paid.

He picked up the pints and turned to go, but Auntie Sheila took his arm. She was a larger than life character with a beehive hairdo that was more than twenty years out of date, but Andy had always loved her uncomplicated directness, her winning smile and generous heart.

'How's your love life, Andy? I was really sorry when you and Susan split up. You seemed right together.'

'These things happen, you know,' he said, diffidently.

'You've got a lot going for you. You'll be alright love.'

She smiled at him again and he took the beers back to his table.

'There you are, Mr Ormondroyd, a pint of bitter. I don't suppose it's quite like the beer back home though.'

'No. I don't suppose it is.'

'Still, you'll appreciate it all the more when you get back home. A decent pint of Yorkshire bitter, I mean.'

'Aye. I'm not that fussed as it happens.'

'What do you mean?'

'Well, there's a lot of splother about Yorkshire beer. I think I'm better off with a southern pint. More beer, less froth.'

He sipped his pint in silence.

'Oh, right. Well…I wondered if I could ask you a few questions about your life in the coalfield? Fifty years is a long time down the pit. No doubt you take pride in having been a Yorkshire miner.'

Albert Ormondroyd eyed Andy.

'No.'

'No?'

'Bloody terrible way to make a living.'

'Well yes, I know how hard it can be to make a living out of digging coal, but there's some sort of nobility in manual labour. Did you always want to go down the pit? I mean, miners have to be a tough breed of men don't they?'

'Aye. That never really interested me.' He paused. The lunchtime drinkers had all gone and the club was silent.

'You know what I always wanted to do? I wanted to be a librarian, but me mam said no, I was to go down t'pit like me brothers.'

This was not quite what Andy had anticipated. The narrative he had had in mind was not unfolding.

'Still, Yorkshire must mean a lot to you, all the same.'

'Well, it's my 'ome right enough.'

'Yes and there's…well, there's Yorkshire cricket, for example.'

'I like cricket well enough, but I don't see that there's owt special about Yorkshire cricket. Just eleven cricketers who 'appen to come from Yorkshire. That Boycott one – he were the worst. Selfish as the day is long. Took a leaf from Maggie Thatcher's book long before there were a Maggie Thatcher.'

'Well yes, but generally speaking, Yorkshire must have a special place in your heart.'

'Aye. Since it's th'only place I've ever lived. Never

been outside Yorkshire before, except once – day trip to Skegness when I were fifteen. 'Orrible place that were, too. This is t'first time I bin down south. Pit villages look much the same as home, mind.'

There was a long silence during which Andy realised that he didn't yet have much to write up in a human interest feature. Then Albert Ormondroyd spoke.

'I always been interested in stories, you know. Always liked books. And cameras – always interested in photography too. I were the first to buy a Box Brownie in t'village. Perhaps I should've been a photographer come to think on it. Any road, I always had me snaps printed at chemist and put them in albums. Album upon album I've got. I looked through them all the other day, right through from the 1940s to the present day. I were looking for the story, you might say, something that made some kind of sense. D'you know what?'

'What?'

'It made no sense at all. Complete waste of time.'

*

Jack returned a little after three o' clock and Andy went to the bar to buy them all another round.

'How did you get on with Uncle Albert?' asked Auntie Sheila.

'Just my luck.'

'Didn't you get on?'

Andy shook his head.

'We got on fine, he's a lovely man, but he's a self-deprecating Yorkshireman. Not only that, there isn't a trace of machismo or chauvinism in him. What editor is going to want to print that? Not mine, for sure.'

# 9

## September 1986

It was the epitome of a small provincial town and the local newspaper where Andy worked as a junior reporter was a typical small-town paper, with its tiny office in a shop near what might have been regarded as the town centre.

It was his first job and he'd only been working there a couple of years, but certain things were quickly becoming apparent to Andy. The newsprint revolution had entirely bypassed this particular publication. In fact Andy wondered if the paper hadn't pretty much missed out on the industrial revolution as well. Everything that was done there was done because that was the way it had always been done.

Modest though its circulation was, the paper played an important part in local life and it reported on everything from Sunday League football to flower and produce shows.

Andy was crouched intently over the keyboard of his electric typewriter, carefully bashing out each individual letter and wishing that at some point in his life he had learned to touch-type. Suddenly, a large pile of envelopes, several inches thick, landed on his desk. He looked up to see Norman the post-boy rummaging in his postbag for any other correspondence he might be able to offload onto Andy's desk.

'Morning Norman, how are you?' he asked and immediately regretted his mistake.

'Generally I'm keeping very well,' said Norman, 'but I did have rather a disturbed night on Saturday. My sister believes it may have been a bilious attack and has advised me to begin a course of bismuth tablets.'

By nature, Norman took a very literal approach to life. If someone asked Norman a question it was plain to him that they must not only want to know the answer, but would also require as much detail as he could provide. The notion of social etiquette never entered his head. Care was needed when talking with Norman and the unwary could find themselves engaged in prolonged, yet largely inconsequential conversation.

Ironically, while Norman was called the post-boy he was clearly no longer a boy in the literal sense. Small and thin, Norman would never see forty again. His hair was cut short yet remained unkempt, his tie – which he insisted on wearing each morning beneath a somewhat moth-eaten sleeveless jumper – was always askew, his collar was often awry and he gave the general impression of being a minor character from a Dickens novel.

It was rumoured that Norman had failed his

probationary period of employment at the paper, but nevertheless continued to come into work even after his dismissal. In the end the editor, Walter Gow, just gave in, kept this quixotic figure on and there Norman had remained for year after year.

To Andy's relief, before Norman could launch into a more detailed account of his ailments, Malcolm Nixon, the senior news reporter on the paper for almost two decades, strolled into the tiny office.

'Uncle Walter wants you to go down to Dover,' he said, as Norman scurried away.

'Why?'

'To run a piece on the ferries – a few hundred words and some decent photos, so get Barry to go down too.'

'What's the story?'

'Nothing really. He wants a puff piece, so dig out some positive figures about passenger numbers, employment and so on. Try to get an interview with the Chief Exec of one the ferry operators, that sort of thing.'

'Why a puff? Can't they pay for advertising?'

'I think Walter's in Round Table or Rotary or whatever it is with some of these characters. He's just eager to please.'

'I sometimes wonder if he knows what he's doing.'

'Oh I don't think he does, not even for a moment. That's not surprising really.'

'Why?'

'Don't you know? His background's not in journalism at all. He's an actor. Used to be in rep. The rep closed and he ended up here.'

'How has he lasted twenty-five years then?'

'I told you, he's an actor. He just acts the role.'

'What?'

'He doesn't know what to do and he hasn't learned much over the last two decades, so he just puts on a performance. He acts out the role of editor. He's quite good at it. He's a bit like the kind of guy who wants to be thought of as the life and soul of the party, so he ends up wearing a Christmas sweater and comedy slippers. You know, the type of bloke who has what he thinks are hilarious slogans on his t-shirts – but they're all in lieu of having an actual personality. It's called faking it.'

'What about professional standards?'

'They're irrelevant, because Uncle Walter is from the age of the gentleman amateur. Your generation has been brought up with the idea that professionalism is a quality to be aspired to, but it's not so long ago that being a professional was considered rather vulgar.'

'Really?'

'Oh yes. Even after the last war they continued with football and cricket matches between Gentlemen and Players, in other words amateurs versus professionals. It was the amateurs who were the glamour boys, not the professionals.'

*

So, a few days later Andy found himself riding his Vespa down Jubilee Way to the Port of Dover. Suddenly, as the road cut its way through the cliffs, the vista opened up and Andy could see the full panorama of choppy grey water, with a ferry nosing through the harbour mouth en route to distantly visible Calais. As he left the shelter of the cliffs Andy felt the wind catch his scooter and he had to strengthen his grip on the handlebars to hold it straight. He rode through the town, then up the Western Heights to one of the ferry companies' sleek corporate headquarters.

When he arrived in the chief executive's suite of offices, Barry Macken, the paper's photographer, was already there and Brian Stephenson, the ferry company's CEO, was obligingly striking a series of heroic poses: gazing out to sea, the landlubber as experienced mariner; at his desk surrounded by papers, chin resting winsomely on his hand, the astute manager; and perching on the corner of that desk with a beaming smile, the picture of smug self-satisfaction as far as Andy could see. This impression was further endorsed by Stephenson's immaculate suit, hand-stitched shoes and dashing, if incongruous hat, which he insisted on wearing throughout the photoshoot.

Once Barry had headed back to the newspaper office to develop the photographs, Stephenson hung up his hat and Andy finally understood its purpose. Apart from the flowing locks at his temples, which were perfectly groomed, Brian Stephenson was entirely bald. He sat back in his throne-like, leather swivel chair and scrutinised Andy closely. Not a word had been spoken when Stephenson raised a pudgy finger and pointed it across the desk, directly at Andy's neck.

'I hope that is not an indication of your political sympathies,' growled Stephenson.

Lost for words, Andy looked down and noticed that the tie he had – unusually – decided to wear to work that day, was bright red.

'It's just a tie,' he said ingenuously.

'Take a look out there,' Stephenson demanded, abruptly changing the subject.

Andy gazed out through the vast, panoramic windows past the hoverport and the Western Docks railway terminus toward the Eastern Docks, where queues of cars and HGVs awaited the ferries which arrived and departed metronomically through the harbour entrance.

'What do you see?'

'Dover beach…Dover harbour,' Andy corrected himself.

'I'll tell you what you see. Free enterprise in action. When the public sector dominated this industry, cross-channel traffic was slow and inefficient. We've proved you can speed the process up and carry huge numbers of passengers and vehicles, all driven by a healthy profit.'

Andy looked out of the window again.

'Turn round!' yelled Stephenson.

Andy jumped.

'Yes, turn-round,' the CEO continued, 'that's where we started maximising the margins. The shorter the time taken to turn the ship around, the more sailings each day, the larger the profit. That's enterprise.'

Andy looked down at his blank notebook, but Stephenson was warming to his theme.

'We're going to diversify.'

'Oh?'

'Yes. Hotels, restaurants – fast food! Do you know what the average hungry British day tripper wants most when they arrive in Calais?'

'A meal in a French restaurant?'

'Burgers!'

'Really?'

'A burger and a pint of British lager. So we're opening our first fast food restaurant, called The Burgers of Calais.'

Andy smiled, thinking this reference to Rodin's sculpture must be a joke. Stephenson though, began to believe his vision was starting to impress, so he went on.

'And our top of the range burger will be called The Keys to the City.'

'Isn't that rather bad taste?'

'It'll taste great, in as much as a burger ever tastes of anything.'

There was a pause.

'Then there are the trains, of course,' Stephenson continued. 'The railways need a dose of private enterprise too. Privatise the railways and I guarantee there will be greater efficiency and lower fares in no time at all.'

'I can't quite see how that would work.'

'Competition! What comes from competition?'

Andy needn't have worried that he was struggling with the impromptu oral examination he was being subjected to, because Stephenson was determined to give away all the answers.

'Enterprise! Enterprise, which demands efficiency and which results – most importantly of all – in profit.'

'You would have different private railway companies, in direct competition?'

'Yes.'

'Different companies' trains competing on the same part of the rail network?'

'Well…no, obviously not, but they'd be private companies. So, there'd be real enterprise.'

'How would they be competing then?'

Undaunted by the apparent contradiction, Stephenson launched into a new diatribe about water, gas and electricity.

'So would each company provide water that is unique to them?'

'Oh no.'

'Customers would be able to choose their water company then? They'd all be competing on price?'

'No, no. Nothing like that.'

The look on Stephenson's face suggested that Andy was being obtuse, but Andy wondered whether this man who ran a ferry company was even fit to run the boating lake on Ramsgate's West Cliff and more pressingly, how he would be able to write the type of story that his editor wanted.

# 10

## March 1987

'Rubbish!' said Mrs Sacke.

Mrs Sacke was the secretary of the local art society and she clearly held strong views about what she called 'modern art'.

'What exactly do you mean by "modern art"?' Andy asked her. 'When did the modern era begin, in your opinion? Is it a 20th century phenomenon, for example?'

She looked at him blankly.

Andy felt he needed a quote from an official of the art society for his article, so he persevered.

'What I'm trying to find out is precisely how you define "modern art".'

'Rubbish,' repeated Mrs Sacke.

'I mean, if we're talking about 20th century art there's Picasso, Braque, Leger, Dali, Nash, Piper, Mondrian, Bacon, Warhol, Freud, Hockney…'

Mrs Sacke pinned Andy with a sharp glance and cleared her throat to speak.

'All rubbish!' she said, loudly and clearly.

It was about 7.30pm that Friday evening by the time he managed to slip away from the art society's annual exhibition, but Andy still decided to head back to the office, because he wanted to file his report. He could hardly call it a review, because he was fully aware that it would have been impolitic to write anything that was less than flattering about the exhibition. Why was it, he wondered, that so often artists' sense of their own worth was in directly inverse proportion to their talent? It had been a relief to leave early.

As he walked along the almost deserted high street he saw two small figures approaching in the gloom. Too late, he realised as they walked beneath a street light that they were Norman and his sister. There was no time for Andy to feign interest in a shop window or turn up one of the narrow side streets and anyway it was clear that he had already been spotted.

'Good evening,' Andy said as they converged.

'It may seem so at present, but I do believe we may shortly have some rain,' Norman replied. 'The barometer was very low before we departed, but as I said to my sister, we really must go to the Conservative Association wine and cheese evening, so we require gaberdines and at least one umbrella in case we encounter precipitation.'

'Well, quite. I mustn't detain you then.'

'Oh, you haven't. We have plenty of time before they start to uncork the bottles of Blue Nun.'

'No, I know, it's just that I need to go back to the office.

I want to write up my piece about the local art society exhibition.'

'In which case I suspect you will encounter Mr Nixon there.'

'Malcolm? It's not often he works late and certainly not on a Friday evening. He's normally down the pub by this time. Do you know what he's doing in the office?'

'I believe he is researching a story.'

'A story? What story?'

'The sinking of a cross channel ferry.'

'When?'

'This evening.'

There was silence. Andy struggled to comprehend this information and its implications. It couldn't have been a joke, even one in bad taste. Norman didn't make jokes.

'You're saying a cross channel ferry has just sunk? Out of Dover?'

'No, Belgium. It was sailing for Dover and it has sunk.'

'That's awful. It's incredible.'

'No, I believed it immediately Mr Nixon told me. The sources of the original report are very reliable apparently...'

'Sorry, got to go.'

Andy turned on his heel and sprinted down the high street, turned right and raced up to the front door of the newspaper office. He turned his key in the lock and burst in. Malcolm was on the phone. He looked grave, pensive and he gestured Andy to sit down with a nod of his head.

After a couple of minutes Malcolm put his hand over the mouthpiece and turned to Andy, who had never seen him look so pale and solemn.

'The *Herald of Free Enterprise* has capsized just out of Zeebrugge. It happened about half-six. I had a call from a mate of mine at Dover Harbour Board. All hell's breaking loose there, apparently. Get down to Dover and get me what you can before the nationals come down from London. I want all the local angles, mind. Give me a call – from a phone box, if necessary – with an update, every hour.'

'A capsize! Is it serious?'

'Of course it's fucking serious!' said Malcolm and started speaking into the phone again.

\*

When Andy looked back in later years, he was never sure what it was that he expected to see that night as he entered Dover. A town in chaos, perhaps, the streets full of people, against a backdrop of wailing sirens and blue lights.

Instead there was an eerie calm. There were no Hollywood-style dramas visible at the Eastern docks. A ferry was making its way out of the harbour towards Calais and there was barely any traffic driving along Townwall Street, the road which ran parallel to the sea. Andy didn't see a single person until he had left the Vespa in the Russell Street car park.

It was still strangely quiet, but small groups were forming as figures slipped out of the shadows. Andy walked down to the offices of Townsend Thoresen, the ferry company which operated the *Herald of Free Enterprise*. The street was empty apart from a group of around twenty people, mainly relatives of crew members, who had gathered outside and were talking in low voices.

A man joined the group and the others turned to him, expectantly.

'Can't get nothing. They won't tell me a thing.'

'Maybe they don't have any news.'

'It's been on TV, so someone knows something. They're just not telling.'

'Bastards.'

A woman started to cry in low, racking sobs, gulping for air in between each one.

Andy knew that one of his duties as a professional was to acquire an emotional distance from what was happening and at least attempt to interview some of these people, but he just couldn't bring himself to do it. Instead he wandered back towards the seafront. Coming in the opposite direction was a face that, even in the dimly-lit street, he recognised as a journalist on one of the other local papers.

He had his ear to a radio, but he looked up and saw Andy.

'Have you been up to the ferry office yet, Andy?'

'Yes, but there's no information coming out of there. The relatives are in a state of shock. What are you listening to?'

'Short wave radio. I'm listening in to the rescue services to get some idea of what's happening and I'm in contact with the Press Association too.'

They started to walk together back along Russell Street.

'What's the latest, are there any fatalities?' asked Andy.

'Plenty. It sounds really grim. What I don't understand is that they keep talking about the bow doors.'

'How do you mean?'

'They say the bow doors are open. The ship sailed, but it looks like the bow doors weren't shut.'

'Doesn't make sense. Why would they do that?'

'Dunno, but it's a question to ask the company.'

They arrived back at the little crowd outside the offices, which had swelled to around thirty, the sound of spasmodic sobbing still in the air. The relatives quickly gathered around the journalist with the short wave radio, desperate for any news.

Andy spent a long night outside the ferry company offices, as the crowd of relatives and reporters grew. At one point it looked as if there might be a disturbance, as a *Daily Mail* photographer snapped a picture of the *Herald of Free Enterprise* on the wall in the offices. The flash went off and there was an instant reaction.

'What the hell do you think you're doing?'

'Got to make a living, love.'

'You bloody vulture.'

For a moment it seemed things would turn ugly, but suddenly everything subsided. This was a congregation overcome with fear and grief, not a violent mob.

Information trickled through during that long night, most of it arriving initially via short wave radio and as dawn broke it was clear that this was a major disaster. Andy decided, after he had phoned Malcolm for the final time, that he would walk up to the Western Heights to get a full view of the harbour, as if that would somehow give him any insight into what was happening across the channel in Zeebrugge. Mostly though, it was to clear his head. All his professional instincts dictated that he should have been filled with excitement about such a major story breaking on his patch. As it was, Andy just felt sick.

In that pale grey dawn it was hard to determine where the sea ended and the sky began. Andy trudged up towards the Western Heights, the most heavily fortified site in Britain during the 18th and 19th centuries. Now it was largely overgrown, it had returned to nature and apart from the old gateway to Archcliffe Fort there was little visible evidence of the former stronghold.

The roads were quiet, but Andy noticed a sleek black Jaguar slide by and pull into a private car park. Even in the murky morning light, he could easily identify the figure who climbed out of the back door. It was the hat which gave him away. Without thinking, Andy jogged across the road.

'Mr Stephenson. Morning. Andy Gibbons, the journalist who interviewed you last September.'

Gone was Stephenson's flashing smile of six months earlier. He looked pensive, hunted.

'Oh yes,' he said eventually, 'you came up here didn't you? I'd hoped for something more from the piece I must admit.' He started to walk away.

'Mr Stephenson, I wonder if I could ask you a few questions about the sinking of the *Herald of Free Enterprise*.'

'No, no it's not appropriate for me to get involved. There'll be a public enquiry in due course, I don't doubt.'

Stephenson started to walk a little faster and Andy accelerated to keep up with him.

'One of the things that will have to be examined by an enquiry is the safety procedure in all ferries. Do you think safety may have been sacrificed for fast turn-round aboard the *Herald*?'

'I can't say.'

They had now almost broken into a trot.

'What about your own ferries, Mr Stephenson, do you think you may have reduced safety in return for operational efficiency? Will you be making changes?'

Stephenson stopped abruptly and turned on Andy with a dangerous look in his eyes.

'Listen sonny, if there are any problems – and I'm not saying there are – they emanate from the errors of individual crew members backed up by a union which is determined to cripple this industry. Now I know your editor personally and if you print one word of this conversation, not only will you be sacked, but I will come round and insert a copy of your lousy rag right up your fundamental orifice.'

Stephenson turned and walked briskly away.

'What about the Channel Tunnel?' Andy called after him. 'Won't that put even more pressure on the ferry companies' profit margins and result in even lower standards?'

But Stephenson had gone.

# 11

## October 1988

This, according to Mike, was the place to be. Andy had been a little uncertain.

'Soho?' he had queried when Mike called him, 'Isn't that a bit, well, sordid?'

'You are so out of date and so provincial,' said Mike.

'Just like you until three months ago, when you suddenly acquired a metropolitan patina. Where is it you live again?'

'Oh, just somewhere south of the river, but I'll be moving soon. To Islington maybe? Though that's a bit leftie.'

'Just like you used to be.'

'There are these amazing buildings going up in the old docklands now, some real investment opportunities.'

'By which you mean houses and flats.'

'Yeah, but a house is not just for living in, is it?'

'Oh, I'd misunderstood. Ever since you and I built houses out of Lego on the dining room table, I'd laboured under the misapprehension that houses were for that precise purpose.'

It had been an exchange typical of their inconsequential fraternal squabbles.

Now Andy stood outside *La Grenouille Jaune* in Dean Street and looked up and down the road for his little brother. When he finally arrived, claiming that he was just 'fashionably late', it became clear that Mike was in the process of another metamorphosis. He had grown his hair long at the back while the top had recently been blow-dried into a luxuriantly bouffant style and he affected the smart-casual mode favoured by the current batch of pop stars and some of the younger television presenters. Yet Andy recognised the jacket, of which the sleeves were studiously rolled up, as one that Mike had bought a couple of years earlier in the sale at Deakins' Gentlemen's Outfitters in Canterbury.

Andy thought his brother looked like the proverbial dog's dinner, but not much worse than the bright young and not-so-young things who packed out the interior of *La Grenouille Jaune* that lunchtime, with their broad shoulder pads and puffball skirts.

'This place is the dog's bollocks,' said Mike.

'I was thinking something about dogs too, but never mind that now. It's an unexpected pleasure to be invited to lunch by you. To what do I owe the honour?'

Mike looked sly.

'Yeah, I was just thinking that as it's my birthday next month you might pay the bill. You know, as a present, in advance.' Mike smiled his winning smile.

Andy sighed and shook his head. 'OK.' He had grown used to his brother's modus operandi.

'Great. Thanks. So, how's life treating you? Broken any big stories? Any scoops?'

'Well, it wasn't a scoop, but the *Herald of Free Enterprise* disaster was the last really big story in East Kent.'

'That was ages ago. It's all done and dusted now.'

'Not really. Certainly not for the families involved. They still have to deal with the loss of their loved ones. Nearly two hundred people died. Knowing that their deaths were avoidable obviously makes it that much more painful for them.'

'What do you mean? It was an accident.'

'In as much as it wasn't deliberate, yes, but it's not like it was an act of God. The deaths were caused by negligence, which is why my articles have been campaigning for a change in the law. We need something like corporate manslaughter to be put on the statute book.'

'What?'

'Well, if a company knowingly sets up systems which are inadequate to protect its customers or its workforce, responsibility shouldn't just lie with those on the front line, but with senior management, right up to the chief executive.'

Mike looked concerned.

'Doesn't sound like a good idea to me.' He paused, looking troubled for a moment, but then brightened. 'Still, it makes you think, doesn't it? We're all right there under Anne o' Cleves' sword.'

'Damocles. It's Damocles' sword. Don't ask, it doesn't matter. What's your point?'

'Well, you know, none of us knows when our time will come and it makes sense to plan for the future.'

'I see.'

'So, I guess now is a good time to talk about your future.'

'Mine?'

'Yes. I mean, have you thought about life insurance?'

'Enough to know that I don't need it. At least, certainly not right now.'

'Why not?'

'Have you noticed that I have no wife and no children?'

'Not got yourself a fork and knife yet.'

Andy looked uncomprehendingly at his place setting, then back at Mike.

'What?'

'Fork and knife, wife.'

'That's not cockney rhyming slang! You just made it up. If it's big city credibility you're after I suggest you use patois that people might understand. Anyway, to answer your question fully, I don't even have a girlfriend at the moment.'

'Oh, I'm sorry you're not getting the attention from the ladies that you'd like.'

'It's nothing to do with that, I just don't happen to have a special relationship and haven't done for some time, if you remember.'

'Look Andy, don't get me wrong, women are great, but they don't give you the buzz that you get from closing a terrific deal, or buying a really expensive car.'

'Even if you can't afford it, which I reckon you can't at the moment.'

'Especially if you can't afford it.' Mike's eyes shone with delight at the thought.

Andy looked around at the crisp white tablecloths upon which Filofaxes and the occasional cumbersome mobile phone had been laid. This was not a world he was familiar with or felt comfortable in and his little brother's desperation to join it made him feel doubly uncomfortable.

'I just think you need life insurance, that's all.'

'And I think you're currently a life insurance salesman, probably working on commission alone, living in a part of south London so dodgy that you affect amnesia to avoid telling me where it is.'

'Everyone has to start somewhere. The guy I work for, John Stamp, has a big house, a Porsche *and* a Ferrari, a blonde girlfriend with amazing...'

'How do you know all this?' Andy interjected.

'Oh, he comes into the office and tells us. All the time.'

'Well this character John certainly believes he lives up to the meaning of his name.'

Mike looked confused. 'I don't get it.'

'He obviously thinks he is what his christian name means.'

'A toilet?'

'Are you serious? No, of course not! Every given name means something specific.'

'Oh right? What does Andrew mean then?'

Andy paused.

'Strong and manly,' he said rather diffidently.

Mike threw back his head and laughed. 'Go on then, what's John.'

'God's gift. That's obviously what your boss thinks he is.'

Now it was Mike's turn to feel uncomfortable and he decided to change the subject.

'Shall we order then?'

Andy looked at the menu. It was written in a strange amalgam of American-English and French.

'Well I've been looking at the menu, but I can't tell what half of it is. What's a 'jus', for instance?'

'You're the one who did French at school.'

'You did it too, you just didn't bother to learn any. Why would I want juice with strips of Japanese beef and why do I want beef all the way from Japan anyway? And what's a "coulis"? It sounds like some sort of hat.'

'If you don't want it, don't order it,' said Mike airily, showing no sign of knowing the answers himself.

When the food arrived it was artfully presented to cover around twenty percent of the plate on which it was served. To Andy it looked not so much like an unfinished expressionist painting, as one that had barely been started. Mike, on the other hand, was all smiles.

'Amazing, eh? This is the future, Andy.'

'Meals without food are the future?'

'This isn't just a meal, this whole place is a statement about the times we live in. You know, a sort of living manifesto of self-confidence, of self-belief...'

'Well, no-one in here looks short of self-belief,' agreed Andy. 'And what's this sort of foam around the perimeter of the plate?'

'That? That's just foam.'

'Yes, but why?'

It didn't take them long to finish their meals and eventually Andy called for the bill.

When it arrived he read it several times.

'Christ, that's a day's pay and I'm still hungry. What are all these extras?'

'Well,' said Mike, glancing at the list of charges, 'there's two cover charges, a twelve and a half percent service charge…and that one's for water.'

'Water? It's all but free! It comes out of a tap.'

'No, no. This is, you know, designer water. Amazing isn't it?'

'Certainly is. Why no charge for oxygen as well?'

'Look, I'm just really grateful. Thanks.' Mike gave Andy his toothiest smile. 'Maybe we can talk about your future another time then. I'm really on my way up now, you know.'

Andy heaved a sigh and found his newly-acquired credit card.

'Happy birthday, Mike.'

# 12

## November 1989

Andy and Jack were at the bar billiards table in the Bell. Andy miscued, four balls dropped inadvertently in sequence and he added another eighty to his score.

'Shot,' said Jack sarcastically.

'Never could quite understand how this game works. The worse I play, the more I score. Occasionally I manage a decent shot, but then that score is wiped out when I knock over a mushroom.'

'That's the point.'

'What's the point?'

'That there is no point.'

'I thought it was a bar game, not a convoluted metaphor for the pointlessness of human existence.'

'Not sure what that means, grammar school boy, but it's probably both. It's still your shot by the way.'

Andy lowered his cue, drew it back, hesitated and slowly stood up again.

'Bloody hell! It's Mike.'

Jack turned to look.

'It is, but what's he come as?'

Through the door which opened onto the darkened, deserted street strolled Andy's little brother. He could scarcely have looked more conspicuous in the village pub and one or two heads turned briefly to eye him sceptically. Meticulously coiffed, he was wearing a lagoon-blue linen suit, the sleeves of the jacket rolled up, the trousers billowing and voluminous. He scanned the pub and when he saw Andy and Jack his face lit up in a big toothy grin.

'Andy, Jack! Hi, how are you?'

'What are you doing round here little brother? I had no idea you were coming down from London. Have you been home?'

'Just briefly. Mum and Dad said you were down here, so I'm down the old dogs and bears and out the door, you know?'

'Down the what?'

'He means stairs, Jack. He thinks it's cockney rhyming slang, but he hasn't quite got the hang of it.'

Mike ignored them and took a look around. 'Still not exactly great in here, is it? Anyway, exciting news, no?' He gave that big grin again.

'You never used to talk like that when you lived round here,' said Jack, sourly. 'So what's this exciting news?'

'Haven't you heard? It was on the tv earlier. We've done it!'

'Sorry?'

'It's over. The Berlin Wall has finally fallen. We've won!'

'Have we? Who did we beat?'

'No, I mean, capitalism has triumphed over communism.'

'Oh right. What happens now then?'

'Well, you know...' Mike paused for a moment, marshalling his thoughts, '...all those eastern bloc countries, those centrally-controlled economies, become capitalist economies and you know, democracies. Obviously.'

'Democracy is the inevitable result of capitalism, is it?'

'Yes.'

'I don't know if you've noticed what's been happening in China lately,' said Andy, finally joining the conversation, but still a little reluctant to re-ignite the usual trench warfare with his brother.

Mike frowned.

'Well, some of it will take time, obviously, but...' He paused and then brightened. 'The important thing is that soon Russia will become a democracy. Free and fair elections, no more dictatorship by a small elite. No more military threat, because there'll be no point in having nuclear or chemical weapons. No more spies. No more state-sponsored murder.'

'Like Georgi Markov's.'

'You mean the umbrella man? Yes, like his.'

'So simply moving from one of those command economies to a market economy can achieve all that? Well, I won't hold my breath,' said Andy, underwhelmed.

'I think you need a drink, Mike.'

Jack came back from the bar a few minutes later with three pints.

'What's this?' asked Mike.

'Don't you recognise it? It's a pint of lager,' said Jack. 'It's what you used to drink down here. I'm afraid they don't have any of those little Mexican bottles with the lime stuck in the neck that you probably drink these days. Anyway, cheers! Drink up.'

Mike looked a little awkward, but covered it by slipping off his jacket, a move he immediately regretted.

'Bloody hell, look at those braces, Andy! My old man's got a pair of those. His aren't bright red with gold clips, of course. Can't you keep your trousers up then, Mike?'

'It's Mikey now,' he said.

'What?'

'I'm called Mikey now.'

'What for?' asked Andy

'It's shorter, you know, more contemporary.'

Jack snorted. 'You think Mikey is shorter than Mike?'

'Never mind. Forget it.' He looked sulky. 'But I am called Mikey.'

After a brief silence, Mike brightened.

'Anyway,' he said, 'Mikey has news.'

'Have the North Koreans surrendered now?' asked Jack, the sourness returning to his voice.

'Maybe Robert Mugabe's conscience has got the better of him. He's stood down to do voluntary work among the poor and disadvantaged in Zimbabwe.' added Andy, unable to resist joining in. 'Though come to think of it, "disadvantaged" covers just about everyone in Zimbabwe these days, except Mugabe and his family.'

Mike ignored them and said, 'I'm getting married.' He awaited congratulation with an air of consummate smugness.

'Not again! How many times have you claimed to be engaged over the years?' said Jack.

'No, really. I wasn't ready before, but this time – this is it.'

'Yeah, well…congratulations Mike,' said Andy guardedly. 'Where did you meet? Who is she?'

'Zeta Volkova.'

'Not a local girl then. Never run into anyone of that name down here at the Bell,' said Jack.

'She's from an international business and banking family. I met her at a polo match – at the Hurlingham Club.'

'Not the Welfare Club then.'

'How old is she?' asked Andy.

'Thirty-five.'

'Ten years older than you.'

'She's no bimbo, for sure. Anyway, she's had a lot of work done.'

'What sort of work? Tiling re-grouted? Soffits replaced?' asked Jack.

'Cosmetic surgery. You know, a nose job and so on. Anyway, it's not just about looks, she's just, you know, brill in so many ways.'

'In which particular ways is she "brill"?'

'She's kind, she's generous, she really likes me. She's already been good for my business career and she stands to inherit, so even if it doesn't work out in the end it could still be a good investment.'

'You're not even married and you're already doing financial planning for the divorce!' said Andy, genuinely shocked. 'These days everything in life seems to be a simple question of addition or subtraction to you. The rest is mere detail.'

'That's just greedy and cynical,' Jack agreed.

'Oh don't worry, what I achieve will be by my own efforts. I'll paddle my own canoe. I'm a self-made man.'

'Looking at the state of you, that's quite a brave admission,' said Jack.

Mike was nettled.

'You're way off the pace down here, aren't you? There's a whole smorgasbord of opportunities out there you know.'

'Smorgasbord?' queried Jack.

'Norwegian buffet,' said Andy drily, but Mike was still in full flow.

'Times have changed. Don't you realise, self-interest is good now? Greed is actually a positive thing, because it drives the economy. Anyway, I'm thinking about my future. I'm not the kind of guy to let the grass grow under my feet. I don't expect the state to look after me, I'm looking to the long term – and the prospects are looking good.'

'That's a tautology,' said Andy.

'I don't know what that is and I don't need to know. The point is, I'm finally going places.'

# 13

## June 1990

Mike and Zeta's wedding was a very strange occasion. It was held, for some reason, in a Scottish castle and no expense had been spared in letting the guests know that the Volkov family was very wealthy indeed.

The bride arrived in a gilded coach drawn by eight white horses. The train of her dress stretched for many yards and tiny page boys, of whom there appeared to be scores, were forever tripping over it. As the bride and groom emerged from the chapel, a hundred doves were released into the highland air, though the precise symbolism escaped Andy. He preferred to think of it as the start of an upper-class pigeon race.

The reception took place in a marquee of hangar-like dimensions. There were five hundred guests, but just one from Mike and Andy's Kentish childhood, apart from their parents, of course, who looked distant and detached throughout. Dorothy Gibbons had been particularly excited about the wedding, but in the event it proved a long and difficult day for them.

Andy was not quite clear what cousin Jack had done to merit his invitation when so many others had been left behind. However, once the reception had begun, Jack busied himself with attempts to engage in conversation some of the many well-maintained women of a certain age, all of whom were wearing – as Andy and Mike's father might have observed – very expensive frocks.

Andy enquired about his cousin's success in this enterprise as he and Jack refilled their glasses at an immaculate bar, which gleamed with highly polished glasses and groaned under the weight of a quantity of luxuriant foliage.

'Not great. Even if I pass the eye contact and smile tests, once I open my mouth to speak I'm as good as finished. How's life with you, Andy?'

'Job's OK. Quite like living in my own flat.'

'Girls?'

'No-one really serious since Susan.' He paused and continued with a sigh. 'The ones I have been out with only seem to see whatever it is they want to see in me.'

'What do you mean?'

'It's like they're looking for me to fill in the bits of their own lives that are missing. Some imagine I'm on my way to becoming an award-winning journalist and like the idea of reflected glory, some think I can introduce them to the social whirl of the media, some seem to believe I can give them the education they never had and some just see me as a meal ticket. I can't be any of those things even if

I wanted to. I'm just a reporter on a local newspaper, but I'm sometimes left with the sense that I'm appearing in a movie version of my own life and I'm not even its central character.'

'They don't just want you for your body then? Never mind, Andy mate.'

They both laughed, drained their glasses and filled them again.

'So it's all about the career at the moment then. You going to get a better job, maybe in London or one of the big cities, make progress?'

'Ah, the myth of progress!'

'What do you mean?'

'Don't you think we all delude ourselves about what the future is going to be like? Most of us don't have the imagination to envisage it as anything other than pretty much like the present, but with the bad bits left out. It's the myth of progress and I'm not buying it.' Andy thumped his hand on the table to emphasise the point. He was not used to drinking champagne, but he ploughed on headily.

'The fact is, I don't believe in all the stereotypical ideas about progress and I'm not even sure if I have any real sense of direction anymore, either.'

'Sounds to me as if you're waiting for that perfect moment which never arrives.'

'What?'

'You know, you think you can't enjoy life properly until it's all perfect. Just doesn't work like that. Remember, things are good for you, Andy. You ought to be pleased, you have a future.'

'I don't seem to be wired like that.'

'Then that's your other option – take it easy. Let time trickle through your fingers occasionally. Remember those Sunday afternoon walks we used to go on with the families sometimes?'

'Over the downs and along the old railway line?'

'That's it. Remember how you used to walk with us most of the time, usually near the back, but when it came to a hill you didn't slow down. In fact you speeded up, you were off ahead, at the brow of the hill in no time.'

Andy thought about it. 'You're right. I never could saunter for long.'

'You've got a sense of direction alright, but you can't get there instantly, so you might want to think about doing a little more of that sauntering of yours from time to time.'

Andy thought about this as their glasses were refilled again and they drank.

A great shout of laughter suddenly went up from a group of the younger guests.

'All the bright young things,' observed Andy. 'It's a bit like a Waugh novel.'

'Which war – first or second?'

'No, the author, Evelyn Waugh.'

'Who's she?'

'It doesn't matter. I do wonder how my little brother gets on with this lot though.'

'Trouble with Mike is, he'll either end up a millionaire, or behind bars.'

They both laughed, but in spite of their intoxication Jack's careless phrase was one which Andy was to have cause to reflect upon in the years to come. For now though, all that seemed significant was an increasingly inebriated assessment of their fellow guests.

'These people are yuppies. You know, the social climbers, the biggest snobs of all. The thing that'll attract my brother is the fact that they've got money.'

'Yes, I reckon these people all have places in the country,' said Jack, swaying slightly and steadying himself against the table.

'I've never seen anyone quite like any of them before and we live in the country.'

'No, no, not that sort of countryside. Not a place where people make a living from the land. Not places like ours. They just about tolerate farmers, but they certainly don't want miners!'

'What do you mean?'

'I mean that the countryside is becoming a sort of theme park for the wealthy and I bet every one of them is a whatsit…you know, one of those people who tries to stop any building anywhere near where they live.'

He knew the word, but it took Andy a while to search the champagne-soaked recesses of his brain.

'You mean a NIMBY! I think it stands for 'not in my back yard'.'

'That's it.'

'You know what, I was actually reading about this recently and you know who came up with that phrase?'

'No.'

'A government minister. A bloke called Nicholas Ridley, but the thing is he's a NIMBY himself. He had a property in some village, but he didn't want any houses built anywhere near it. They only want development if it enriches them and if it's a long way away from where they live.'

There were more gales of laughter at the far end of the marquee as a couple of smartly-dressed young men dunked a third in one of the illuminated ornamental fountains.

Jack and Andy re-filled their glasses.

'See that couple over there?'

'Her with all the jewels?'

'That doesn't narrow it down much Andy.'

'Bet they love a few peasants in their country retreat, especially if they can't read or write properly. How rustic they must seem! But most of all, how sophisticated and superior they think themselves by comparison. The only people they really want to know are the ones who are as similar to them as possible.'

Jack laughed out loud at Andy's drunken outburst, glancing over his cousin's shoulder at the young man in his soaking morning suit now hauling himself out of the fountain and swinging wild, drunken punches in the general direction of his tormentors.

'I expect that when they leave the city they just pack the green wellington boots and strap a green plastic nose to the car's radiator grille.'

'What?'

'Well…you know Red Nose Day, Jack?'

'That comedy thing?'

'Yeah. They've made red noses for the front of people's cars for that now.'

'I've seen some. Daft.'

'Well ever since the European elections last year, when the Green Party got a lot of votes, people have started

88

attaching green noses to the radiator grilles of their cars, to show that they care about the environment I suppose.'

'But they're made of plastic. It's, you know, a petrol-based product.'

'Exactly! Sheer stupidity.'

They both laughed raucously, emboldened by the alcohol. A few heads swivelled to look in their direction.

Then Andy felt a hand touch his sleeve gently and he turned. It was his mother.

'Hello Mum.' He smiled a drunken smile at her.

'I've asked them to call a taxi. I'm going to take your father back to the B&B, Andrew. He's feeling rather tired.'

He glanced over at his father, who seemed a strangely isolated figure with an unhealthy pallor and Andy started to sober up almost instantly.

'OK Mum. I'll explain to Mike, if he asks me.'

He knew Mike wouldn't though.

# 14

## December 1990

The phone on the bedside table in Andy's flat suddenly rang out in the dark. He fumbled for the light, switched it on and saw that it was a quarter past one. He picked up the heavy receiver, dropped it on the floor and then retrieved it.

'Hello?'

The voice at the other end was familiar, but somehow distant.

'He hasn't moved for three-quarters of an hour,' came his mother's voice, softly, but insistently. 'I tried to wake him, but he wouldn't wake up and he hasn't moved since.'

Andy's mind raced.

'Dad? Do you mean Dad won't wake up?'

'Yes, of course. He was making this terrible noise in his sleep. A terrible noise like he couldn't breathe. I tried to wake him, but he won't wake up.'

'Dial 999, call an ambulance. I'll be round as soon as I'm dressed.'

*

Ken Gibbons had never been a religious man, but Dorothy had insisted on a traditional funeral at the village church.

'What would people think if we didn't have a proper vicar and a church? He was a manager at the colliery, you know, until last year when the pit closed.'

Dorothy's own faith was a curiously one-dimensional affair. She would have classed herself as a Christian, an orthodox Anglican, neither high nor low church. She had booked her passage to the after-life, but seemed content with steerage rather than Port Out Starboard Home, not least because her attendance at the village church did not extend beyond weddings, christenings, funerals and the occasional Christmas carol service.

Other than Jack and his family, there were few other mourners at the graveside that December afternoon, as the light drained from the winter sky. Ken had been management, so there were no ex-miners present and his contemporaries in the office were either already dead, or preferred not to be reminded of the last miserable years of mining in Kent. Only Sally, one of the secretaries, was there, wearing an inappropriately short leopard-print skirt, her hair newly dyed peroxide blonde, to mark the solemnity of the occasion perhaps.

Also absent from the graveside was Mike, who absolutely had to be in New York, apparently.

'Forasmuch as it hath pleased Almighty God of his great mercy to take unto himself the soul of our dear brother, Kenneth Arthur Gibbons, here departed, we therefore commit his body to the ground,' intoned the priest, as crows in the trees surrounding the churchyard raised the volume of their cries.

'Earth to earth, ashes to ashes, dust to dust; in sure and certain hope of the Resurrection to eternal life, through our Lord Jesus Christ; who shall change our vile body, that it may be like unto his glorious body, according to the mighty working, whereby he is able to subdue all things to himself. Amen.' There was a muttered, stumbling 'Amen' in response and figures began to drift away in the fading light.

Andy and his mum stood in silence, alone at the edge of the grave. Then Dorothy who had remained silent and stoical with hands clasped and eyes lowered throughout the service and interment, spoke softly, as if to herself.

'I wish I'd not said those things to him now.'

'Which things?'

'It was after he was made redundant from the pit and took early retirement. He was always round the house, under my feet. I couldn't stand it. I said, "Ken, since you've retired you never go to work any more. Never!" I always used to say that. I wish I hadn't.' For the first time she seemed close to tears.

'Come on mum, let's go home.'

He took his mother's arm and they began to walk back towards Andy's car. They were intercepted on the church path by the vicar, who seemed determined to tick off the last of his tasks for the day.

'Mrs Gibbons,' he said, grasping her hand and keeping hold of it, 'I am so sorry for your loss. Mr Gibbons lived a valuable life. He was a good man, was he not?'

Dorothy thought for a moment and then looked intently at the vicar.

'Well rector, he always had clean, pressed underpants.'

The two of them, Andy and his mother, set off again down the path, leaving the vicar to contemplate this idea.

# 15

## January 1991

Mike and Andy sat side by side in the waiting room, until they could meet the family's solicitor to discuss probate. It seemed as if the legal business had not been especially prosperous in east Kent of late, because the office was decidedly run-down. It gave the appearance of having been created by knocking together several terraced houses in the town centre. The interior was dim and the sunlight that did penetrate the windows on that bright winter morning was freighted with dust.

They sat in silence for a while in the empty brown waiting room. Then Mike spoke.

'Great about the World Cup.'

'That was last summer.'

'I know.'

'When did you start becoming interested in football… or any other team sport for that matter?'

'It's what it stands for.'

'Cheating on an international scale?'

'No, no. How it transforms, you know, how people behave. Our national character.'

'Really?'

'Brilliant semi-final.'

'We lost.'

'Yeah, but that bloke…Gaz?'

'Gazza.'

'Yes.'

'Paul Gascoigne.'

'That's him.'

'Those tears. Top drawer.' Mike leaned in, confidentially. 'We're all allowed to be in touch with our feelings now, us men. We have permission to cry. It's become sort of heroic!'

'I think the only feeling Gascoigne was in touch with was his own disappointment that he'd be suspended if England made the final. Those tears weren't altruistic, they were about him feeling sorry for himself.'

'Still, comes in handy,' said Mike, a sly look coming over his face. 'Used it on Zeta the other night – worked a treat. Took her completely by surprise. Turned the tables on her.'

'Is that indicative of the foundations on which your relationship is built?'

'I reckon I could use it in business too, if things got tight. You know, if all else fails, turn on the waterworks. Probably still works better for women, but at least we men have a chance now.'

Andy shook his head.

'I sometimes wonder if you and I really are related.

Now would be a good time to find out if we're not. You know, before we go in to see the solicitor.'

All was quiet, except for a clock ticking somewhere in another part of the building.

'You may have a new-found interest in football, but I'd hate to play the game with you, Mike.'

'Why?'

'You don't understand team sports, do you? You just do what you want. If I looked for you on the left wing you'd be far out on the right hand touchline, pleasing yourself. Then you'd invent some sort of spurious justification for it.'

'You don't understand. It's the spirit of the times. You should try being a bit more like that, my old dinner.'

'That last sentence didn't make any sense.'

'It's rhyming slang, dinner plate…'

'Mate? No, it's china plate, as in "my old china". You really ought to give this stuff up if you can't do it properly. It doesn't make you sound any more like a Londoner, it just makes you sound like a poseur.'

'Listen, the point is that I live by the spirit of the times and that spirit is all about enterprise right now.'

'What you do is enterprising? Bursting into tears in order to manipulate someone is enterprising? It just looks self-centred, it's avaricious and avarice doesn't need any encouragement, because – in case you hadn't noticed – self-interest is already built into human nature.'

'You're saying I'm greedy, because I have aspirations?'

'What aspirations?'

'I want to be number one.'

'At anything in particular? And what would that give

you give you that can't have now?'

Mike thought for a moment.

'Brands! I want to be able to afford all the biggest and best brands.'

'What for? Why will they be better than things that aren't branded, or the things you already have?'

'I don't want what I can already have. I want more than that and if I can get it then that means I'm entitled to it. That's all.'

'Oh listen Mike, I don't really mind. As long as you pay your taxes you can roll in cash and consumer goods for all I care.'

'Taxes?' Mike looked incredulous. 'Taxes are for the little people, Andy, that much we know. My accountant ensures I have as little to do with taxation as possible.'

It was Andy who gently broke the surface of the sea of silence that followed. His thoughts had turned back to their father.

'I sometimes can't help feeling that Dad died believing that all the things he worked for hadn't really turned out the way he'd expected, that they'd sort of withered away over time.'

'What do you mean?'

'He worked for the National Coal Board from the time he came out of the army. Coal was king in those days, the country depended on it. Dad believed in it and he believed in what he was doing. For him it was another type of national service, if you like. He worked his way up in the NCB, it was the centre of his life and now it's all as good as gone. I don't think he felt he understood the world we live in today.'

'Yes, you've got to be ready to duck and dive these days. No good getting stuck in a rut like Dad did.'

'He did what he thought was right, but what did he have to show for it?'

'Well, he paid off his mortgage.'

'What?'

'He told me last year. With his redundancy money he paid off the last of the mortgage on the house.'

'So that's all he had to show for forty-five years work? He died safe in the knowledge that he wouldn't be pursued by some celestial debt recovery agency for defaulting on his mortgage repayments.'

# 16

## February 1991

There had been a light covering of snow overnight and the little yard behind the newspaper offices reflected a strange, ethereal light into the editor's office. In this tiny room at his even tinier desk sat the editor, Walter Gow, the numerous ridges and furrows of his large, jowly face dramatically lit.

There was a knock on the door.

'Come!'

Andy slid into the room and stood there, in front of the desk.

'Sit down,' said Gow.

This was not a given. Andy had conducted numerous meetings and received occasional dressings-down in this office in the standing position.

Andy sat and waited in the silence.

Suddenly Gow flourished a piece of paper with the

panache of a conjuror concluding a trick by producing a white rabbit.

'What is this?' he asked in his deep baritone voice.

'I imagine it's my letter of resignation.'

'Why?' Gow knitted his eyebrows in theatrical perplexity. 'Why would you want to leave?'

'Well, I've been here for more than six years and I suppose I want to take the next step in my career.'

'You want to throw away the prospects you have here?'

'I'm not sure what you mean. There are no vacancies coming up on this paper. Malcolm is a really good journalist, I've learned a lot from him, but he's not going anywhere.'

'Things are not what they were,' Gow mused, shaking his head sadly. 'In years gone by youngsters would join a company and remain loyal to them for the rest of their working lives.'

'It's not disloyalty Mr Gow. I'm grateful for the chance you gave me and I like working here. I care about the paper's reputation and its importance to the local community. I grew up round here, so it's my local paper too.'

'Then why leave?'

'I have opportunities and I want to take them. I want to turn freelance.'

Gow grunted.

'I'm not sure your experience will be sufficient for the nationals. They'll need a bit more than you have. Exposing dirty vicars, or shop assistants with their fingers in the till is about as intense as it ever gets around here. All the same, you've got to learn your trade somewhere and here is as good as anywhere.'

'As you know very well I've already written a few pieces for the nationals. You seemed to like that at the time, because our paper got a namecheck…and most of the fee as well. Remember, each piece I wrote was on local issues: pneumoconiosis and other types of lung disease in ex-miners; safety failures on board cross-channel ferries…'

'Yes and as a result of that article people like Brian Stephenson won't talk to me any more.'

'Isn't it worth it to expose the truth?'

'Young man you have a lot to learn. This business is not about truth it is about entertainment. Readers want to be entertained and ideally they would like their prejudices to be confirmed too.'

'I don't agree. I think there is a market for honest journalism. If you pander to the lowest common denominator then you will end up with a country full of idiots.'

Gow was silent. He looked peevish before growling his next sentence.

'Have you any freelance work?'

'Actually yes, I'm due to write pieces for *The Times* and *The Observer*. There are a couple of magazines interested in feature articles too. The world has changed, people no longer spend their careers with one organisation. I need to move on.'

His editor looked unimpressed. 'So what are these pieces about?'

'There's one feature on the Guinness Four. You know the sort of thing – in-depth profiles, trying to understand who they are and what it all means.'

'That big fraud trial last year? All it means is that four individuals got greedy and decided to bend the rules a little. There are codes of conduct in business that have stood the test of time. These were just a handful of rotten apples, no more than that.'

'The trouble with finding rotten apples is that it's a sign that there may be more decaying in the barrel.'

'Poppycock!'

'I'm not so sure. Anyway, I want to see what I can find out. I want to see what I can do.'

There was a long silence while Gow contemplated this statement.

'I'll give you fifty pounds a month. That's a £600 salary increase.'

'I'm grateful for that offer, but it isn't about the money. I suppose I'm like most other people, I want to leave a mark, I want to see what I can achieve.'

Gow looked defeated. Ambition that could not be bought off cheaply was something he did not fully comprehend.

'So be it, Andrew. I wish you well. Close the door behind you.'

# 17

## April 1991

Andy was not looking forward to his long weekend with Mike and Zeta at their London flat.

He wandered a little tentatively into a large, elegant square and eventually found the right apartment. It looked as if every property in this particular neighbourhood would probably command an asking price that began in seven figures. He pressed the buzzer.

'It's Andy.'

'Come on up, big brother.'

Andy opened the door and climbed a wide staircase which swept up to the first floor, where Mike stood in his doorway.

'How are you?'

'Fine. How about you, Mike?'

'Mikey.'

No sooner had they sat down in the ornate drawing room than Mike leant forward confidentially.

'Hey look, big brother, I need to ask you a favour.'

Mike's face was unusually intent, his habitually overactive demeanour momentarily suppressed.

'OK.'

'It's Zeets.'

'Is it? I mean, sorry, I don't understand.' Andy looked baffled.

'Zeta. My wife.'

'Oh. Yes.'

'There's a problem. She's sick.'

'Really? She looked very well when I met her. Not to say, sleek and pampered. I think she told me she has regular health checks somewhere on Harley Street. Have they turned up something worrying?'

'No, no, no – all A1, or whatever it is they say, but…' Mike left a long pause, '…she's ill.'

'Seriously ill?'

'Yah, I'm afraid so.'

There was a longer pause and Andy began to grow restless, as a worm of doubt started to nibble away at his empathy. Mike could, after all, be palatially self-indulgent. It was an unworthy thought and Andy locked it away.

Eventually Mike spoke.

'She drinks.'

'Alcohol? You mean she drinks too much?'

'Not just the usual, Louis Roederer, but Moet, Veuve Cliquot, Bollinger – literally anything she can lay her hands on. And Stolichnaya – she started drinking Stolichnaya. She consumed half a bottle of vodka in an evening before Christmas!'

Andy remembered long sessions in the club, when young men would habitually dispatch fifteen pints and be up again for work the next morning, green and bilious, but present and ready for the pit. It occurred to him that Zeta's might be something of a first world problem, but he persevered.

'What can I do?'

'I've got to go to a meeting in the City.'

'Which one? Oh, you mean the square mile.'

'Exactly. A big deal. Big, big deal. This could be the one. You know, *the one*. Trouble is, it clashes with Zeta's appointment on Monday. She says she needs someone to go with her, to give her moral support. He's very good, her doctor. Top man. Very expensive.'

'She's going to see a therapist and you can't go, because you have a meeting,' said Andy, eyebrows knitted. The penny had dropped. 'So you want me to go instead.'

'Yah. He's a top, top man. Very hard to get appointments.'

'But I hardly know Zeta.'

'You're family, dear brother. Understand? That's what I told Zeta anyway.'

'And she was OK with that?'

'Sure, sure. Once she'd stopped crying. And shouting. You know.'

'I'm not sure about this, Mike.'

Mike fixed his brother with his gaze.

'Andy, I need this. Zeta needs it. It's a matter of great medical importance.'

Andy exhaled gently and gave the merest nod of his head.

*

So it was that Andy found himself sitting next to Zeta in the back of one of the Volkov family's limousines. It was black and shiny and the interior was about the size of the average central London flat.

Andy barely knew her, but if he thought it would be an opportunity to become better acquainted with his sister-in-law he was mistaken. Zeta sat there detached and crystalline. If she really had had all the surgery Mike claimed, the surgeon was exceptionally skilful. Privilege, he decided, has its own elixir of youth.

Nevertheless, there appeared to be a slightly nervous edge to Zeta that early Spring morning as they glided through Berkeley Square and along Regent Street, drawing up in a quiet mews just off Harley Street. This was, Andy supposed, a very important encounter for her.

Zeta darted a glance at Andy. As if reading his thoughts she said, 'I haven't been for saay long.'

Zeta, like many women of her type and education, had a habit of over-extending her vowel sounds.

'I massed my last appointment.'

'Massed? Oh, you missed it. Well, I can understand that might make you nervous. When was your last appointment?'

'A week ago.'

Andy considered this, as the chauffeur took the long walk from the driver's seat to open the rear door for Zeta.

They passed through the classically-pillared entrance of the consulting rooms, with its immaculately polished brass plate. 'Dr Josef Frankl' it read, his name followed by a list of abbreviated qualifications the length of a prose poem.

The receptionist, who emerged from behind a dark wooden desk constructed from most of the contents of a rain forest, looked less like an earthly creature than something that had emerged, already formed, from a Pre-Raphaelite painting.

They were shown into an elegant side room, tastefully littered with very thick, very heavy, very glossy magazines. They were alone and silent. After about five minutes the receptionist led them into Dr Frankl's consulting room. Frankl was short, neatly bearded and looked as if he was auditioning for the part of 'Psychiatrist' in a not especially well-researched TV sketch show.

The consulting room was dimly lit, furnished with three armchairs and a long, studded leather couch which gave the impression of never having been used. The walls were lined with books, which had titles like *Resolutions to Placebo Addiction*, *Homeopathic Treatments for Hypochondria* and *Alcohol: Ten Unique Abstinence Programmes*.

Zeta smiled a warm, yet wan smile at Dr Frankl and introduced Andy as her brother-in-law. They sat and Frankl started to shuffle through a huge sheaf of papers, reading, nodding and occasionally giving a small grunt. A clock ticked noisily in the silence. Eventually Frankl slid his gold-framed glasses to the end of his nose and looked up.

'So. Zeta. Since you last came, how much alcohol have you drunk?' Andy couldn't quite place the accent, but it didn't seem Germanic in quite the way his name suggested.

Zeta looked down into her lap, as if ashamed of her answer.

'None,' she said.

There was a silence as Dr Frankl raised a hirsute eyebrow.

'Nothing?'

'Nothing at all.'

'But you missed your last appointment.'

'I know.'

'And yet you have drunk no alcohol at all in that time?'

Frankl looked troubled. He shook his head and started to scribble furiously.

'This is a serious development,' he said.

The dialogue continued, taking in Zeta's childhood, her relationship with her parents, her relationships with men, her sex life – somewhat to Andy's discomfort – and various apparently random aspects of her medical history, ranging from toothache to pins and needles. Was it Andy's imagination, or did Zeta appear to derive enormous pleasure from this time devoted to talking exclusively about her? Certainly she seemed unconcerned that little mention was made of alcohol, or her consumption of it.

'Well, we are approaching the end of this consultation,' said Frankl eventually. 'As I said at the start, I am concerned that someone with an alcohol dependency as serious as yours has not consumed any alcohol in more than two weeks.'

Zeta looked worried.

'So I propose to increase the frequency of your consultations with me, to once every five days.'

Zeta looked at him intently. 'Thank you, doctor. Thank you saay much.'

Frankl stood up, put down his papers which fanned out on his chair, then showed them both to the door. As Andy passed, he couldn't help noticing that all the sheets of paper appeared blank, save the top one which was a partially completed *Times* crossword.

The huge black car was waiting for them outside, purring almost imperceptibly and they began the journey south in silence.

Head bowed, features in the process of collapse under the weight of impending tears, Zeta wound a small and no doubt exceptionally expensive handkerchief around her fingers. She cut a lonely figure and Andy felt he ought to do something to help.

'I believe the medical profession say that if people moderate their drinking to within government guidelines it can add a couple of years to their life expectancy.'

'Yah.'

'I mean, how would you spend an extra couple of years if you had them?' Andy persevered.

Zeta was silent. No thoughts, it appeared, had crossed her mind.

'Well. I rilly like cocktail bars. You know, the fashionable ones – exclusive, upmarket.'

Andy winced inwardly at this paradoxical aspiration, but he was still determined to help if he could.

'I just wondered,' he said, 'if you haven't had a drink for over a fortnight and you don't particularly miss it, if one way of dealing with your problem isn't just to continue that way. You know, just carry on not drinking.'

Zeta, vulnerable and doe-eyed a few moments before, suddenly straightened her back, turned her head and fixed Andy with a piercing look.

'How dare you!' she hissed.

'I'm sorry?' Andy was cowed by this sudden, unexpected development.

'I am seriously ill. I have needs.'

'I know, I just thought it might be a solution to your problem.'

'I don't want a solution. I want support.'

She glared at him a little longer before turning her head away and remaining silent for the rest of the journey, save for a few barely suppressed sobs as they approached Belgravia.

# 18

## April 1991

The door opened and Mike bounded into the room. It is possible he could have looked more pleased with himself, but Andy couldn't imagine how.

'How did it go then?'

'Massive,' said Mike. 'It's going to be massive. Hardly any upfront investment. Huge, guaranteed returns right from the get-go. Big offices just off Threadneedle Street. The lot. Clive and Roland – they're my business partners – say I'm going to have some sort of portable computer too, an Amstrad!'

Oasis Investments, it appeared, were going to be at the cutting edge, leaders in their field. Mike continued in this hyperbolic vein for five minutes, eventually pausing for breath.

'Mike...'

'Mikey.'

'Don't you want to hear about how it went with Dr Frankl?'

'Sure, sure. He's the top man you know. Says Zeta is very interesting.'

'I think that might be a euphemism.'

'What? I thought that was something to do with assisted suicide.'

'Never mind. Look, I'm a little concerned about him.'

'He's the top man,' said Mike, adding a little unnecessarily, 'he's a doctor after all.'

'He is. Have you read the brass plate outside his consulting rooms?'

'Yah,' said Mike enthusiastically, 'shed load of letters after his name!'

'Which qualification impressed you most?'

'Well, all of them. He's got more letters after his name than anyone I've ever heard of.'

'Perhaps, but his doctorate, for example, is a ThD.'

'There you go. Told you. He's a ThD.'

'Yes. It's a Czech qualification. It means he's a Doctor of Theology. I expect he'd make a good vicar, but his medical expertise probably doesn't extend much beyond going down to the chemist to pick up a prescription.'

Mike thought about this. 'She's getting better. Dr Frankl is making her better,' he said.

'Yes, from what I gather she's not had a drink for weeks and very little since the turn of the year. Shouldn't she just continue, you know…not drinking?'

'Zeta needs to be cured. The doctor is curing her.'

'What's he curing her of?'

'A disease. She's got a disease.'

'Really? What disease?'

'It's got a name. A Latin name.' Mike folded his arms triumphantly.

'What's that then?'

'Er…*Bibens Nimis*, I think.'

'You didn't do Latin at school, did you Mike? What *Bibens Nimis* means when translated is, "drinking too much".'

'So?'

'Well, couldn't she just stop drinking too much, or even give up drink altogether?'

'Look, the doctor is curing her.'

'How do you know?'

'He's the top man. Very expensive.'

'But is he any good?'

'Of course. I told you. He's very expensive.' Mike paused. 'You might think about consulting him yourself, if you had the money. I've seen the amount you drink in the Bell or at that miners' club.'

'You think I'm suffering from *Bibens Nimis*?'

'Yes. You probably are.'

'I don't think so.'

'There you are,' said Mike, his triumphant tone returning, 'you're in denial!'

'What do you mean "in denial"?'

'Those who won't face up to their drinking problem are in denial.'

'If you extend the logic of your statement that means the entire population is in denial, other than the few problem drinkers who own up to their problems. All the teetotallers, all the moderate drinkers will deny it, so that technically puts them "in denial" along with those problem drinkers who won't admit they've got a problem.'

There was a silence while Mike thought about this. He started to colour up. It was an interesting shade of vivid pink which Andy recognised from their childhood. Then Mike stood up, the dam burst and it all came out at once.

'You think you're so fucking clever with your grammar school education and your Latin and your "it's a Czech theology degree". Well what are you? A fucking reporter on a fucking local paper. That's all. Just you wait until I make it big. And I mean seriously big! Then we'll see who's really got what it takes. We'll see what's really worth something in today's world.'

He remembered to slam the door as he left the room.

# 19

## December 1992

Andy was suddenly woken from a reverie by the strident ringing of his new mobile phone. He picked the lump of black plastic from his desk and put it to his ear.

'Andy Gibbons.'

There was a pause and then he heard his mother's voice.

'I'm alright dear,' she said. 'I'm fine.'

Andy's heart sank. It was perhaps the fifth time that week she had called to share this news with him. It was clear from her tone that what she felt was more or less the opposite of what she was saying.

'I'm going to be just fine.'

'I know Mum. You will. Is there anything I can do for you?'

There was another pause.

'I need some custard creams.'

'What?'

'You know – little biscuits.'

'Yes, I know what custard creams are.'

There was silence, as if Dorothy was collecting her thoughts.

'It's your brother… Michael… I'm worried about him.'

'Why?'

'I never see him.'

'He lives in London now, Mum.'

'He doesn't call. He's changed. A mother has to worry you know.'

'Well don't worry, Mike is fine,' said Andy, not quite convinced of this himself.

There was another silence.

'But I haven't got any custard creams.'

'Look, shall I take you shopping after work?'

'What time?'

'After work, about 5.30.'

'Lovely. What time did you say?'

'About 5.30.'

'Won't the shops be shut then? Can't you come now?'

'I'm working. The Safeway supermarket is open late tonight, until 7.'

'So what time are you coming round?'

'5.30.'

'Hang on, I'll just write that down. Andy coming at…'

'5.30.'

'5.30?'

'Yes.'

*

They had strolled solemnly up and down the aisles under the harsh neon lighting of the supermarket, occasionally stopping in their tracks so Dorothy could gaze at some random article. They finally arrived at the till with an eclectic, not to say eccentric basket of goods. There were custard creams, of course, though Dorothy had had to be reminded about this central purpose of the shopping trip. There was cat food, although she had no cat. Apparently one of the cats from the nearby farm could sometimes be enticed inside the kitchen with a saucer of cat food. Then there was a pair of shoe trees, some liver salts and various random articles which had been on special offer.

At no point had the question of Mike been raised and Andy did not mention his name, because Dorothy seemed to have moved on from the worries that had afflicted her earlier in the day. Others, however, had replaced them. Dorothy had suddenly stopped in the middle of an aisle.

'I want to be cremated,' she said.

'What, now? Shouldn't we wait until after you've passed on?'

There was a time, not so long ago, when Andy would have been told not to be so facetious, but now his mother just looked at him, apparently unable to understand why he would not simply comply.

The cashier put the items into a plastic bag for her, but when it came to the moment for Dorothy to pay she looked startled, giving the impression that this was an unexpected development to which she had no useful response. Andy looked at her, as if for the first time in years. His mother's eyes were both vacant and troubled – there was almost a hunted look. Her face had become sharper and more lined and her hair, he noticed, was a flyaway mass, dyed orange-brown, through which long grey roots clearly showed. Andy leant across and silently gave the cashier his money.

\*

Once he had dropped his mother back at the family home, helped her unpack the shopping and made sure she had something for her dinner, Andy drove back to his flat in the town in his newly-acquired VW Golf, trying to decide what to do next.

Uncharacteristically, he decided to call Mike and talk to him about what might be best for their mother.

It was Zeta who picked up the phone.

'Hello Zeta, it's Andy.'

There was a silence.

'Andy Gibbons. Your brother-in-law?'

'Oh yes! Andy. Hello, how are you?'

'I'm fine thanks. And you?'

'Not saay good.' As ever, Zeta was stretching her vowel sounds as far as they would go.

'I'm sorry to hear that. What's the problem?'

'You remember I had that issue…with alcohol?' she said hesitantly.

'Yes. Have you gone back to drinking?'

'Oh no, no. Well, I haven't touched any alcohol for a year and a half.'

'Great. Well done. So, what's the problem?'

'Well it seems I have a deep psychological need for something to replace it, for a surrogate as it were…because I've developed another addiction.'

'Oh dear. I'm sorry to hear that. What is it you've become addicted to?'

'Evian.'

'That's mineral water though. Surely that's OK isn't it?'

'No, no, I've been drinking litres of it every day. Sometimes I mix it with elderflower cordial.'

'That sounds fine to me.'

'I am afraid not. Dr Frankl says I have developed a dependency. I need further treatment.'

Was it class, age, gender or something else that made Zeta so dogged in pursuit of personal problems that barely had any objective substance, Andy wondered briefly.

'Zeta, is Mike there?'

'No. Mikey is in Hong Kong.'

'Oh, what's he doing there?'

'I really don't know. He never tells me these things and I never ask.'

'I see. What must it be like for you to be burdened by such an enquiring mind?' he said and instantly regretted it.

Zeta, though, appeared to remain unaware. She lived in a world of her own devising, in which she was the only inhabitant.

# 20

## January 1993

Andy had arranged to meet his brother in an Italian restaurant in Wardour Street. Mike had not been impressed by the venue, but he was there on time all the same, fashionably dressed, well-groomed and tanned. Even his designer sunglasses, perched on his forehead, did not seem out of place, which was a little surprising given that the sun had not made an appearance all day.

'So, you've been in Hong Kong, Mike?'

'It's Mikey.'

'You've been in Hong Kong? Mikey.'

Mike brightened at the mention of his preferred style of name and grew more animated.

'No, no. I've been in Dubai.'

'Zeta said you were in Hong Kong.'

'No. Dubai. She must have gotten confused.'

'Gotten?'

'Yah, I mean Hong Kong was great in the eighties, but it's a bit passé. Dubai is the happening place right now.'

'Really? I thought it was mainly desert.'

'No, they've got massive plans for development there, which they're going to trial soon.'

'By the noun trial you presumably mean a verb like try or test?'

Mike ignored him and pressed on.

'There was a problem in that part of the world two or three years ago with some war or other, but they're bouncing back now and it's all about buying cheap and selling expensive. You know, building in added value.'

'You're talking about the Gulf War.'

'Yah, big plans for golf courses and loads of other leisure facilities too.'

'No, no. The *Gulf* War. That's the war you were referring to. There was never a war about golf, as far as I'm aware.'

'Oh, right. Anyway, these people think big and there are some massive construction projects being talked about. It's the future.'

'And Hong Kong isn't?'

'Not any more. We're going to let the Red Chinese take over there, apparently, so that's hardly going to be good for entrepreneurs like me. I can't actually believe we're giving it to them, but I guess no-one saw it coming. We need to get a bit of backbone in this country, you know. Thatcher would never have allowed it. Would've sent a task force, or something.'

'I think we've all seen it coming. Hong Kong was only leased to the UK by the Chinese and the lease expires in four or five years.'

'But it's part of Britain.'

'Geographically, legally and historically it's part of China.'

'Anyway, doesn't matter, Dubai's the place to be now.'

Andy was silent for a while, formulating a question.

'Do you remember when we last went to London with Mum and Dad? You were about twelve.'

'Vaguely.'

'You wanted to go to the Tower of London and we'd not been there long when you said you wanted to go to see Big Ben. When we got there you said you couldn't wait to visit the Planetarium and when we were there you decided that what you really wanted was to go to Madame Tussauds. There wasn't time to go anywhere else after that and I'm not sure how much you really enjoyed it, but you went on about how you couldn't wait to come again, even though you were already there.'

'So?'

'Just wondered if that memory rang any bells.'

'No,' said Mike, showing not a flicker of interest. 'Why would it? It's the past.'

*

Mike had insisted that they went back to 'his club' after the meal. It wasn't one of the strictly formal, traditional establishments in the Mall or St James's, but it was still clearly expensive and exclusive and Andy wondered what kind of strings Mike had had to pull to get himself elected.

'A little better than the Welfare Club, eh Andy?'

'Except that the price of a drink in here would probably buy you several rounds back home.'

'You have to critique everything don't you?'

'If you mean criticise, no, but I will offer you a critique of the way in which you are determined to turn nouns into verbs: it's pointless; it's unnecessary; and it's a waste of time which only detracts from what you are trying to say.'

Mike looked sulky, but he bounced back, determined to press home his point.

'This place is quality though. It's got class.'

'If you say so. It occurs to me that the Marx brothers were right though.'

'Not bloody Marx again!'

'Do you mean Karl Marx?'

'Obviously.'

'He would have been the least funny of the Marx brothers. What I was actually referring to was Groucho's remark about not wanting to be a member of any club that would have him as a member. Or even one that would have my brother as a member, from my point of view. Anyway, how did you manage to get yourself elected?'

'Clive and Roland know some of the key members. In fact some of them came round for dinner at the flat a couple of weeks ago.' He broke off. 'It didn't go so well, actually.'

'Oh, why not?'

'Zeets got very upset. Ran off to her bedroom.'

'Why?'

'Well I needed to sort out the thing with Roland. It had been bugging me.'

'What thing?'

'I've been watching them at social occasions for some time and I think – well I know – he fancied her and she probably fancied him too. You know, her self-esteem is quite low and everything. I think he'd been propositioning her.'

'Really? Could just have been some sort of harmless flirtation, surely. What happened?'

'Oh, I managed to get him on his own and I just told him she was really shit in bed. You know, not worth the trouble. It got back to her somehow, unfortunately.'

'No wonder the poor woman has low self-esteem,' said Andy, feeling an unexpected pang of sympathy for Zeta.

'Look, Mike, I wanted to talk to you about Mum. I'm worried. I'm not sure she's coping on her own and we need to decide what to do.'

'Oh, right. Well, whatever you think.'

'No, we need to make this decision together, because in a few years residential care might be the only option.'

'Well, if that's what you think.'

At that moment Mike's mobile phone rang.

'Yah. Oh, hi Clive. No, that's fine. OK, I'm on my way.' He turned to Andy. 'Sorry big brother, another time. Got to go.'

And with that he was gone. Andy paid the bill.

# 21

## July 1993

'I've got a spare rod for you,' said Jack.

'No, it's alright,' Andy replied, struggling to raise his voice above the noise of the wind whipping in off the sea.

'Why not?'

'I'm just no good at it.'

'You might catch something.'

'Last time I caught the back of my neck.'

'What?'

'I was casting, but instead of casting my line out to sea I embedded the hook in the back of my neck.'

Jack tried not to sound too scornful in his laughter.

The two of them sat side by side at the end of Deal pier, watching the waves crash on the steep pebble beach. The wind was getting up and dark clouds were driving in from the south-west.

'What have you been trying to catch?'

'Mackerel, mullet, pollack. I've caught sole here in the past too.'

'And what have you caught today?'

'Nothing worth keeping. I've thrown a few dabs back.'

'I'm bound to ask why you do it.'

'Well, one answer would be that it's better than installing radiators.'

'I guess it must be.'

'And it's therapeutic. I can put my mind in neutral out here.'

Andy looked at the dark, angry sky and the churning grey sea and decided that it wasn't a form of therapy that he would find very restorative. He watched a lone gull flying into the stiff wind, attempting to beat its way along the coast, but making little progress.

'I've had a serious think about leaving and starting again,' said Jack.

'I always thought it would be me who would go, not you.'

'I've told you Andy, you've got it made. Steady job, your own place, a car, a few pints down the Bell or the club, game of cricket on a Sunday...'

'Well as a cricketer I'm mediocre at best!'

'Mediocrity has its own advantages Andy mate. If you get a few runs – you know, a half-decent innings – you're buzzing for a week. People like Billy and Kenny need to rack up a ton before they get excited. They've got real talent. You know, not enough to play professionally, but enough to be better than most of us. Poor sods, it must be frustrating for them.'

The only sound was the 'melancholy, long, withdrawing roar' of a breaker on the beach while Andy thought about this idea. Jack interrupted his reverie.

'So anyway, I've decided. I'm going.'

'For good?'

'Yes, I've had enough. It's hand to mouth, I work six days a week, I've no real ties…apart from you.'

'And the rest of the family.'

'They don't need me any more. I'm going up north.'

'Yorkshire?'

'County Durham.'

'That's almost off the map. Why there?'

'The uncle of someone the Yorkshire lot know. He's got a little electrical business up there and he's due to retire. It's not much, but at least I'll start with some customers. I never wanted to be a heating engineer.'

'I thought the bloke you work for said there were good prospects for you down here.'

'Ha! He's told me lots of things which turn out not to be true. He's always saying that he's too honest for his own good, but he's a liar. In fact it's not a bad rule of thumb, Andy. Pay particular attention to people who tell you they are no good at lying.'

'Why?'

'They tend to be liars.'

Spots of rain, borne on the wind, were starting to fleck the pier's concrete bulwarks.

'A bit like my little brother then.'

'Why?'

'Oh…I don't trust him any more.'

'No one ever trusted Mike. He's always lived in a world

of his own, but he's harmless enough, isn't he? He's just a fantasist.'

'That was probably true at one time, but he's got himself mixed up with people who I'm not sure are good for him. I worry that he's in over his head. His business partners are a couple of ex-public school chancers who are only out for themselves and I really don't understand how his marriage to Zeta works either.'

'Does he ever talk to you about that stuff?'

'Not really. That's Mike, I'm afraid. He has the capacity to compartmentalise, to box up and lock away things that might otherwise trouble him. It's no solution. The problem just re-surfaces long afterwards when he eventually opens the box again and discovers that it's all gone rancid inside.'

# 22

## November 1993

Andy had agreed to meet Mike in a large pub near Victoria station. It wasn't one of those characterful 19th century urban drinking barns, but a drab, dimly-lit tourist trap full of perfunctory brewers' Tudor and faux-chalked blackboards offering fish and chips and the roast beef of Olde England. It reeked of stale beer.

'Why did you want to meet here?' asked Andy once Mike had finally slid in by a side door and found his brother in a corner illuminated only by a large fruit machine.

'Well, I thought it would be convenient for you, up from Kent by train and all that.'

'It's not your usual style. It lacks a degree of panache, does it not?'

'Well yes. As it happens, I'm not keen to bump into anyone I know.'

'Why?'

'I have problems.'

'Go on.'

'It's not worked out the way I anticipated. The business, you know. I mean, it seemed like a great opportunity, but things have gone a little…sour.'

'What's the problem?'

'We can't pay out any more.'

'Can't pay out?'

'To the investors.'

'But you've been making big money. You said so yourself. I've seen you lighting cigars with £50 notes, though God knows why – you don't even smoke! Just look at your car, your suits, your…whole lifestyle.'

'I'm worth it.'

'You're not worth it if you can't pay your investors.'

'OK, OK, but things have happened so fast. It's just that we can't pay out all of a sudden.'

'Why not?'

'We're not getting the return on the investments.'

'Have you tried going back to the bank and asking to borrow more?'

'We tried, but they were worse than useless. There were too many conditions, too many restrictions on a further loan. They're too closely regulated, the banks. They need to change – to understand that you have to speculate in this world, take a few risks.'

'What about the Volkovs?'

'I can't.'

'Why not?'

'I just can't.'

'Oh, alright, what about other backers then? There

might even be some sort of support from the public sector, I suppose.'

Mike laughed, mirthlessly.

'That's a joke. I tried all the government departments I could and ended up being referred to some local council way out in Cambridgeshire somewhere.'

'What? I mean, why?'

'It's where our company's registered office is.'

'Where, exactly?'

'Er…I think it's called Whizz Bitch or something.'

'Wisbech.'

'Oh. Means nothing to me. Anyway, I spoke to some clown called Henry Lord in the economic development department. He kept asking me where the public benefit would be in a loan to our company. I assured him the money would be well spent, but it made no difference to him.'

'When did it all start to go wrong?'

Mike shook his head, as if haunted by the memory.

'It wasn't long after Clive and Roland brought in Buttplug O'Neill.'

'I don't believe it!'

'No, seriously, he was Marketing Director.'

'I mean his name. If that really is his name I wish I'd been at his christening, if only to see the vicar's face.'

'That's his name as far as I know. It all seemed to be going so well too. There was a big uptick in sales and then all of a sudden we couldn't pay out.'

'You say you're not getting the return you need on your investments. Which particular ones do you mean? Has there been a crash in the market?'

There was a long silence broken only by the hum and squawk of the fruit machine and a mournful clicking of forks on plates as diners searched for nourishment among the remnants of the roast beef of Olde England.

'Oasis never had any investments,' said Mike softly.

'What?'

'I mean, I thought there were. You know, to begin with. The trouble is it's a competitive market and everyone wants an instant return on their money these days.'

'Short-term commitment and the myth of easy money – they're toxic and they're everywhere nowadays. So what do you mean "there were no investments"?'

'Clive and Roland assured me that there were investments – top of the range investments. The best. Really innovative. Ahead of the curve. The sort that no-one else is really buying into yet. Massive returns. Huge profits. But there weren't any. It turns out they never existed.'

'A Ponzi scheme! You're part of a Ponzi scheme.' Andy took time to assess the gravity of this news. 'You could be in big trouble, Mike.'

Mike looked down at the soggy beer mat on the table in front of him.

'I am in trouble. We're being investigated by the Fraud Squad. They'll almost certainly press charges.' Suddenly a whining, pleading self-pity set in. 'Why is this happening to me? I mean how can it be wrong to make money? We're just trying to make something of ourselves, to show a bit of enterprise, it's just self-help…'

'It certainly sounds as if you've all helped yourselves. Have you ever considered the consequences for the investors who pay into a scheme which takes their money and doesn't pay out? Not least because it never could pay out! I noticed a while back that Oasis Investments' parent company is called Mirage Holdings. Is that some sort of public school joke? Steal people's money and laugh at them at the same time.'

'Look, if you don't want to help me, just forget it. Go back to Kent. Doesn't matter.'

'No, no. I can see now why you couldn't go to the Volkovs for support. Obviously I'll help. What can I do?'

Mike brightened a little.

'My lawyer thinks my best chance is mitigation. He suggested I looked around for medical opinions that might help, so I immediately thought about Dr Frankl.'

'The old charlatan that Zeta consulted?'

'Look, if you don't want to help...'

'Go on, go on. You know I'll help if I can.'

'Well I went to see him and all he could offer at the start was self-esteem.'

'Self-esteem?'

'He's an expert in self-esteem.'

'Yes, I got that impression too.'

'The idea was that low self-esteem would be part of my mitigation and Frankl would write a report to that effect, but now he's come up with something better. I'll need treatment, so if I take an intensive premium course with him, he believes he could diagnose a much more powerful mitigating condition.'

'Does he have a menu card? Or particular conditions that he likes to pair with specific offences, like some sort of gourmet tasting menu?'

'I'm serious Andy. This could help me out of a massive hole. I'm looking at a custodial sentence here.'

'I know. OK, what do you want me to do?'

'I want you to come with me to my next consultation.'

'Why not take Zeta?'

Mike paused.

'Zeta…doesn't know. I've been waiting for the right moment.'

'Oh dear.'

There was a long silence.

'I don't think that was his real name by the way,' said Mike, eventually.

'What?'

'Buttplug. I think that might have been a nickname.'

'Give me strength!'

# 23

## November 1993

Andy's second visit to the consulting rooms of Dr Josef Frankl took place in circumstances a little less comfortable than the first. They had decided to take a taxi, rather than the limousine, in order to avoid provoking questions from Zeta. The first real storm of the autumn was brewing and it hurled the detritus of London's streets at them as they made their way through Portland Place.

Frankl showed no sign of remembering Andy from his first visit two and a half years earlier, but the doctor impressed upon him the importance of the complete confidentiality of the consultation. He went through the whole pantomime psychiatrist routine, complete with long pauses and sudden, unexplained questions or exclamations. Andy could see that Mike was entirely engaged with the performance, concentrating intently on Frankl's every word.

Eventually Frankl remained silent for about two minutes, staring at Mike.

'In my considered, professional opinion,' he said eventually, 'you are bipolar Mr Gibbons.'

Mike looked stunned. Then he reddened and managed a stammered reply.

'I-I-I-I'm sure I'm not. I've never had any sort of physical interest in men, you know. I'm 100% heterosexual.'

'I think you misunderstand. I believe you suffer from an illness that brings severe high and low moods, together with changes in sleep, energy, thinking, and behaviour. People who have *bipolar* disorder can have periods in which they feel overly happy and energized and other periods of feeling very sad, hopeless and sluggish. It is a relatively recent term for a condition that used to be known as manic.'

'I see.' Mike's mind was beginning to function again. 'And that will help in court will it? In mitigation.'

'As long as you can demonstrate that you are going to undergo a thorough treatment programme with the right specialist practitioner. Yes, I think so.'

'The right specialist practitioner?'

'Me. Or if that is not admissible by the court, someone I recommend. It is a specialised field.'

'Ah, of course. Doctor, may I be excused for a moment? I'm sorry, I think it must be the stress.'

'Naturally. The restrooms are along the corridor on the right.'

Mike departed and Frankl and Andy were left examining one another in a profound silence. It was Andy who broke it.

'Impressive qualifications,' he said.

'I'm sorry?'

Andy glanced down at his reporter's notebook, in which he had quickly jotted down Frankl's qualifications when they arrived earlier.

'On the name plate at the entrance.'

'One must study to achieve the necessary level of competence.'

'Well you certainly give the appearance of having done that. First and foremost, you have a Thd.'

Frankl observed Andy and remained silent.

'I live in Kent and I was reading in one of the local newspapers about a priest who came to speak as a guest preacher at a service in Canterbury Cathedral. He was Czech and he was there to give a sermon about the revival of religion in the country after the break-up of the Soviet bloc. He had a Thd too.'

Still Frankl said nothing.

'What are your medical qualifications Dr Frankl?'

'Spiritual and psychological well-being are closely aligned,' said Frankl, fixing Andy with his gaze.

'Don't come here again,' he added softly, refocusing his attention on his notes before Mike returned to the room.

*

As they were driven back to Belgravia in a taxi, Mike seemed a little brighter and started to talk about the future as if he didn't have the prospect of the court case and a subsequent prison sentence hanging over him. Andy decided the subject needed to be broached.

'You just let Frankl medicalise you.'

'What?'

'You just let him package and label you, even though I don't think you believe for a moment that you are bi-polar.'

'Dr Frankl is the top man. Very expensive.'

'Where would you have drawn the line? Autism, attention deficit hyperactivity disorder, early onset male menopause…'

'Shut up Andy.'

'Maybe it's an idea for a new game show. You know: "I'm offering you ADHD and a year's supply of Ritalin in exchange for your bi-polar disorder!"'

'I don't need this. I stand to go to jail if I can't get the mitigation right.'

'OK, OK. Just so long as you know that this guy is as big a fraud as you and Clive and Roland all are.'

# 24

## June 1994

The three of them were an incongruous sight, sitting in line on a sofa in the offices of one of the most expensive legal firms in London. Andy, Mike and Mike's solicitor, McIlvanney, sat together as the staff glided silently past them. If Mattel had manufactured a Severe Legal Barbie range, then every staff member would have been a suitable model for it. Exclusively female, dark-haired, perfectly coiffed, made-up and coutoured, they looked professionally determined to ensure that Ken's car, Ken's boat and Ken's house were all duly transferred to Barbie in any settlement. Or the other way around, if that's where the money was.

McIlvanney was the solicitor Mike had originally consulted before he was formally charged with fraud. Florid and rotund, McIlvanney was a man who clearly knew what to do with an Ulster fry, Mike had thought when he was first ushered into his office.

'High four hov ye come?' the solicitor had asked.

'Sorry?'

'Just nigh. High four? I mean did yers get the tube or the train or...'

'Oh, I see. No, taxi from Belgravia.'

'Well, sit ye dine,' McIlvanney had said, indicating a chair. 'Tea? Coffee?'

'Tea, please.'

'Kie jeece?'

'Pardon?'

'Kie jeece. Jeece o' the kie.'

Confused by his solicitor's unusual linguistic style Mike had remained silent and then to his startlement McIlvanney had suddenly let out a loud 'Moo!', before saying 'Mulk!' at the same decibel level.

'Oh, milk. Yes please.'

It was the complexity of the case as well as the fact that McIlvanney spoke a variant of English that Mike had not encountered before, which meant he was relieved to be referred on to one of the top legal firms in the City.

Now, outside in the street, the traffic heaved and honked in one of the hottest days of the year. Inside these pristine offices the silence was almost oppressive, the temperature so ambient as to be uncomfortable. They waited for their audience with James Granby QC, who would be acting for Mike at the trial.

'Is Granby any good?' Mike asked McIlvanney, nervously.

'He's yer man,' said McIlvanney.

'He's the top man you mean?'

'Aye, top man,' repeated McIlvanney.

'Very expensive?'

'Aye, but ye get what ye pay for, ye must know.'

'Look Mike,' interrupted Andy, 'what exactly do you need me here for?'

'Granby wants to ask you about one of my expert witnesses.'

'Who?'

'Dr Frankl.'

'Jesus! Well I hope he's not looking for a glowing reference.'

One of the tallest and most forbidding legal Barbies arrived silently above them.

'Mr Michael Gibbons and Mr McIlvanney, Mr Granby will see you now. Come with me, please. Mr Andrew Gibbons, remain here until you are called.'

No-one would have considered disobeying her instructions.

After about twenty-five minutes Andy was called into the meeting. Granby was surprisingly young, dark, perfectly suited. He clearly understood stagecraft well enough to know that in order to command the highest fees he would need to look the part.

'Now, Mr Andrew Gibbons. May I call you Andrew for ease of function.' It wasn't a question.

'Andrew, you – I believe – accompanied Michael to the consulting rooms of a Dr Josef Frankl and you are familiar with his work.'

'Well, a little, I suppose.'

'Would he be a plausible witness?'

'Yes, very. Very plausible.'

'Good.'

'But he's a complete charlatan.'

'Even better.'

'His ideal patients are wealthy people with nothing much wrong with them.'

Mike slid Andy a sideways glance of irritation.

'I do find scruples tend to get in the way in these matters,' said Granby.

'Scruples get in the way of justice?'

'Ah no, Andrew. This is not justice. This is the law.'

'Do you think I have a chance?' interjected Mike, looking a little pale.

'Well, the case is likely to come up before Mr Justice Humphreys,' said Granby, collecting up papers from the desk in front of him, 'and his political inclinations, shall I say, indicate that he might not be as inimical to a little personal enterprise as some other judges. However, we shall see.'

As Granby filled his briefcase Andy's curiosity got the better of him.

'Do you deal with many cases like this each year?' he asked.

'The meter is, as it were, still running,' said Granby snapping his briefcase shut and looking at them enquiringly.

'Come on Andy,' said Mike, grabbing his brother under the armpit and almost dragging him to his feet. 'Thank you, Mr Granby, we've finished.'

*

The three of them found themselves in the cacophonous street, blinking in the strong sunlight and inhaling the thick fug of emissions. McIlvanney turned to Mike and Andy.

'Mr Justice Humphreys, that's just grand. See 'em lodge,' he said, tapping the side of his nose conspiratorially.

'See what?' asked Mike, still somewhat bemused by the meeting.

'Seem lodge as Granby.'

'Oh, same. Same lodge? What are they, otters?'

'Beavers,' corrected Andy.

McIlvanney threw back his head and laughed, his waistcoated belly heaving up and down.

'Masons! They're both Freemasons from the same lodge.'

# 25

## February 1995

'No. Sorry.'

'Please Andy. I need this. I won't ask for anything more.'

'Leaving aside the fact that you undoubtedly will ask for more at some point, I would just remind you that I have already accompanied both you and Zeta to appointments with Dr Frankl and then I went with you and McIlvanney to see Granby. I don't now want to come with you to your Client Preparation Session with Mr McIlvanney, for several very good reasons. Not the least of these is the fact that I'm not the client. You are. More than that though, don't you think it's time you started to stand on your own two feet? Only you can really deal with this situation. You're the one who is going to be on trial.'

There was a long silence during which Andy wondered if he hadn't been a little harsh and Mike embarked on one of his habitual sulks.

'Alright, if that's the way you want it,' he said and rang off.

*

Mike returned to McIlvanney's shabby little office alone and with a sense of profound foreboding.

The corpulent solicitor had added a gold-chained pocket watch in his waistcoat to embellish his ensemble and looked even more like a squire from a Hogarth print than he had before.

'Tea or coffee?' he asked Mike.

'Tea please.'

'High do ye take it?'

'How do I take it? No sugar, just a little kie jeece please.'

McIlvanney looked baffled.

'You know, jeece of the kie.'

'What?'

'Er, I'd like it white, please.'

'Mulk! Ye want mulk! Why did ye not say so?'

As the teas were being prepared, McIlvanney began his introduction to the session.

'Nigh this is to prepare ye for your appearance in court. It is not witness coaching, which I am forbidden to do and yer man Mr Granby has emphasised that there must be no coaching. Is that clear?'

Mike nodded nervously. At that point if McIlvanney had instructed him to give all his evidence in a broad Ulster accent he would have complied. He felt as meek and biddable as he had ever done in his life.

'At the first hearing all ye hov to do is enter your plea. Understand?'

'Yes, yes, of course.'

'Nigh, ye still intend to plead not guilty, am I right?'

'Yes.'

McIlvanney started to make notes.

'At the trial itself ye need to answer all the questions directly, but don't get drawn into debate with the prosecuting counsel if ye don't like his line o' questioning. At all costs try to avoid a direct lie. If the lie is exposed then so are ye and yer case may well be lost.'

Mike nodded feebly.

'Nigh this is important. This here is a complicated case and the more complex ye can make it in your responses the better. Use as much financial jargon as ye can and when ye do, make those answers as long as possible. There's not as many barristers can find their way back through a labyrinth of close financial detail as ye might think. Then there's the jury. They'll have lost the thread after the first few technical terms. Blind 'em with science why don't ye?'

'So, how should I answer when I'm questioned about the Ponzi scheme?'

'By never calling it a Ponzi scheme for a start! Ye'd be admitting yer own guilt. Call it by the fund name yer company gave it. Make that name as long as possible. Maybe abbreviate it later in your evidence so the jury starts to doubt whether it's the same fund as ye were talking about earlier. Mind, I can't be telling ye how to answer questions. It's not right for me to coach ye.'

And so it went on, with McIlvanney 'not coaching' Mike in some detail. When it was over McIlvanney looked Mike in the eye.

'Ye've nat been to prison before, hov ye Mr Gibbons?'

'Of course not.'

McIlvanney chuckled.

'Ah there's many a man sat where ye are, has said the same thing to me before they went inside. Just remember what I've told ye today. Believe me ye'll not be wanting to spend any time in prison, so ye won't.'

As he tumbled out onto the street again Mike felt drained. He looked at his reflection in a shop window and all he could see was a wan, pale face with wide, staring eyes.

Pressure was beginning to build.

# 26

## March 1995

Andy dialled Mike's mobile number and imagined his brother's new custom ringtone, *Moving On Up* by M People, going off at the other end.

'Hello.'

'Oh, hi Mike.'

His brother did not correct him on this occasion.

'Andy. Alright?'

'Yes. I was wondering about you. The trial started today. How did your first day in court go?'

'I changed my plea.'

'What? You pleaded guilty? You've spent months compiling a defence. You're paying crazy money for Granby. What changed your mind?'

'It was on Granby's advice. He thinks my best option is to plead guilty, shift the responsibility to Clive and Roland and rely heavily on the mitigating circumstances.'

'Your bi-polar disorder?'

'Yes.' Mike sounded almost meek. 'I…I just can't face going to jail. I wanted to give myself the best chance of staying out. It's been hell.'

His brother sounded so broken that Andy didn't mention the thousands of investors who had presumably also gone through some kind of hell since losing their money.

'I told you before, it was Clive and Roland,' said Mike, a note of desperation creeping into his voice. 'It was their scheme, I just went along with it.'

'Your head was turned by the prospect of a new Amstrad,' Andy responded, more acidly than he had intended. 'I imagine you're not very popular with Clive and Roland.'

'Christ. You should have seen the way they looked at me in court. I'd really believed they were good men at the start. You know, sound blokes.'

'Why?'

'They were wealthy, they seemed successful.'

'Even if they were wealthy, how would that make them "good men"?'

There was a pause.

'You know. Hard work brings success and being a success is a good thing. It's a virtue, if you like.'

'How about some of the people we grew up with, don't you think they worked hard? They weren't rich though. Or what about Albert Ormondroyd, for instance?'

'Who?'

'That relation of Jack's, from Yorkshire. An entire life working down the pit and nothing to show for it. Look, I'm not preaching,' said Andy, sounding very much as if he was preaching, 'but I think you need to re-adjust your world view. Hard work equals success, which equals wealth, so wealth is thereby a virtue, that's just a development of the old Protestant work ethic.'

'What?'

'Mill and factory owners used to tell their workers that hard work was a virtue in itself, which would be rewarded in heaven.'

'In heaven? I'm not sure that makes much sense.'

'It made sense from the point of view of the owners, but there is no objective evidence to suggest that it had any benefit for any of their workers. Anyway, my point is that all this wealth equals virtue stuff originates from there.'

'Oh, right. I'm not really in the mood for one of your lectures, I'm afraid...'

'Sorry, sorry. I know.'

Andy changed the subject.

'So, what happens with the case now, Mike?'

'There's an adjournment. Then Clive and Roland will be tried and eventually, if they're found guilty, we'll all be...' He tailed off and shuddered. 'Sentenced.'

'What will their defence be like?'

'Same as mine was going to be I expect. Just make the whole thing sound so complex and so technical that the judge and jury lose the thread along the way and don't have enough certainty to convict in the end. A lot of filibustering and detailed technical evidence are what's required apparently.'

'All of which is great for the legal teams who add to

their personal fortunes by the hour, of course. God it's a mucky business.'

'I know, it's a nightmare. I swear...' Mike's voice wavered, 'I swear Andy, that if I get out of this I will change. You won't recognise me.'

'Do you remember Profumo? John Profumo.'

'No, who's that?'

'He was Minister of War in Macmillan's government. Eventually resigned after being caught lying to Parliament.'

'Vaguely. Was that the thing with Christine Keeler?'

'That's it. Well you know what normally happens when politicians are caught lying, or at least, certainly what happens these days. They carry on lying about the lies. They blame everyone but themselves. Or they just keep a low profile and worm their way back into power at a much later date.'

'It's what I'd expect, I guess.'

'An affair and some lies were enough to bury Profumo's career, but nowadays I don't suppose it'll be long before they become qualifications for the highest office in the land. The point is that Profumo acknowledged the gravity of what he had done and withdrew from politics. He has devoted the remainder of his life to charity, working with the poor in the east end of London.'

There was a silence on the line.

'Yes. Yes, that's what I'll do. If I get out of this mess I'll give something back, I'll work for charity, I'll serve the community...'

'Make sure you do, little brother, make sure you do.'

# 27

## June 1995

Mr Justice Humphreys made his entrance, resplendent in full-bottomed wig and raven-black robes. Here the familiar narrative of the great majesty of the law was being played out in a way that, as intended, left the common man in little doubt about his place in the scheme of things. Andy, who sat in the public gallery, felt it keenly in the pit of his stomach and knew that his little brother, there in the dock, would be feeling it far more intensely.

Mike was instructed to stand. He looked small and forlorn amid the panoply of legal might assembled there. The judge leaned forward, slid his glasses to the end of his nose and looked directly at Mike.

'Michael Arthur Gibbons, you have pleaded guilty to the charges brought against you, those of Conspiracy to Defraud, Fraudulent Misrepresentation and Creating a False Instrument. It is now my responsibility to pass sentence.

'These are serious crimes and I would be failing in my duty if I did not pass a sentence which reflects the harm that you have caused. I take into account the fact that you have pleaded guilty and that the individual sums involved were almost uniformly less than £20,000.'

It occurred to Andy that while £20,000 might not be a lot to Mr Justice Humphreys, it may well have represented the life savings of some of the unfortunate investors who had lost their money.

'A custodial sentence however, is mandatory in such cases and this court must be seen to hand down punishment appropriate to the crime.'

Mike had turned white and appeared to take half a step backwards to steady himself.

'I therefore sentence you to two years and six months imprisonment.'

In the silence that ensued it seemed to Andy as if his little brother, standing in the dock facing the judge, was the loneliest man in the world.

'However, we live in an age where enterprise is not only desirable and to be encouraged, but where it is important for all parties, including investors, to fully acquaint themselves with its risks. All too often entrepreneurs find themselves bearing the burden which should be shouldered, at least in part, by willing participants, in this case the investors. This particular enterprise, of course, has proved to be ill-fated, but I am persuaded by the evidence provided by Dr Frankl that you are suffering from...' He paused, replaced his glasses on the bridge of his nose and looked at his notes, '...bi-polar disorder and that this condition played a significant role in your involvement in the crime. You are, I understand, now receiving treatment for this…er…affliction.

'As a result, I have been minded to suspend the custodial sentence and have determined to do so for a period of eighteen months, subject to reparations where practicable, and therefore impose upon you a community service order of two hundred and forty hours.'

\*

When Andy eventually caught up with Mike outside the Old Bailey, he found his brother standing alone on the pavement, breathing heavily.

'You OK, Mike?'

'Yeah. Yeah, I'll be fine.'

'You were hyperventilating.'

'I was just breathing deeply, taking in the air, breathing in the thousand different smells of this city and thinking how different things would have been if the judgement had been a prison sentence instead.'

'Hurrah for masonic cronyism, eh?'

Andy realised that that might have been a little brutal, but Mike wasn't listening. He was looking up and down the street, but clearly not finding what he wanted.

'What's the matter, Mike?'

'I'm just looking for Zeta. I texted her and I thought she might be here by now.'

'Did she reply?'

'Not yet.'

'How has she taken all this?'

'I'm not sure.'

'What do you mean, you're not sure?'

'She hasn't spoken to me for months.'

'No communication at all?'

'Well, she leaves me little notes around the flat sometimes, when she's there.'

'What do they say?'

'Oh just little things like, "you thieving bastard".'

'Not exactly *billet doux* then. Look, I'll buy you a drink to celebrate your freedom, but let's not hang around here with the legal types. Text Zeta and tell her we'll be in the Coal Hole in the Strand.'

Mike was reluctant, but he acquiesced.

'OK. I just wish she was here.'

# 28

## September 1995

Andy felt the chill in the air immediately he stepped off the train and into the gathering dusk at Durham station. He'd never been this far north before and was surprised to discover that winter seemed to have already begun here.

The taxi office found an old Lada to take him out to the village that was his destination and as they drove further and further away from the comforting silhouettes of the cathedral and the castle, perched on its rocky outcrop above the city with the River Wear below, the landscape became more barren and more alien.

In the distance he could see strings of lights straggling across the moors, denoting tiny villages. Beyond them, illuminated by the last rays of sun from below the horizon, the shapeless bulk of old slag heaps appeared, as if to create some rudimentary science fiction film set.

The taxi pulled up at the end of a narrow alleyway in the middle of a village of identical terraced houses.

'Ye gan doon theer an' it's on ya reet, mind,' the taxi driver told him.

Andy walked unsteadily, clutching his bags and the only sounds he heard were his feet negotiating the cobbles. He had not seen another soul since he entered the dark and silent village. He found number 171 and knocked on the front door.

'Will ye go round the back and through the yard? We dinna use the front door,' came a woman's voice from inside. Andy retraced his steps and opened the gate into the tiny walled yard. The back door opened before he could knock and there stood Jack, a big smile on his face. He held out his hand and grasped Andy's warmly.

'Good to see you, Andy. How are you doing?'

'All well, Jack, but I'm wondering if this is the same country I left back in King's Cross this afternoon. Where is everyone?'

'It's a bit different up here,' Jack agreed.

Jack showed Andy through to the kitchen and introduced him to Gill. Andy had heard a little about her, a local girl who had met Jack in one of the nearby pubs. Tall and fair with intense blue eyes, there was something about her that was unlike the village girls who Jack had pursued with varying degrees of success back home in Kent.

'Sorry about making you come in past the netty,' she said, 'but we don't use the front door.'

'Netty?'

'The outside toilet, in the yard. We don't use the front

room much either. It's too cold in winter, so we make our parlour in here. Have a seat.'

'It's very cosy. Thank you.'

The kitchen-parlour was warm after the chill of the evening, but dimly lit. Andy could just make out the garish pattern on the wallpaper which suggested that the room had not been redecorated since the 1970s.

Gill put the kettle on, but Jack offered Andy a beer.

'Brown or Amber?'

'I don't know.'

'Have a 'journey into space' then,' said Jack, handing Andy a bottle of brown ale and a half pint glass.

'Thanks. Cheers. Well, a place of your own, Jack. How are you finding it?'

'Expensive. I mean the price wasn't bad – a fraction of what I would have paid down south. Good thing is, it took longer to get over the property slump round here than it did down south, so prices were already low. Anyway, the old woman who lived in the house had died and her family needed the money, so we got it cheap. It's the mortgage repayments that keep me awake at night.'

'It's not me then, pet?' asked Gill in mock reproach, from the other side of the room.

Jack laughed. 'And you, love. You know that.'

'You're both working though. I mean, you've both got skilled jobs.'

'I know, but it's not the same, being a jobbing electrician. I'd prefer a steady pay packet each month. I never know how much work I'll have – it's almost always too much or too little – and round here there's not much money.'

'He needs to stop doing cut-price jobs for people he feels sorry for,' said Gill, coming over to join them with a cup of tea in her hand.

'And you're a teacher I believe,' Andy said to her.

'Not quite. I'm a teaching assistant at the village primary school. I love it, but they're talking about closing it down.'

'Why?'

'No pit, no work. No work, no young people with families. Simple as that. They'll just let the place die.'

'So it's just to do with the numbers?'

'Everything's run by accountants these days. It's all about the money. I feel sorriest for the kids with special needs.'

'What do you mean?'

'Children with physical and mental disabilities. There are a few in every school and this won't be the only village school to close down, so they'll all be sent to special schools in Newcastle. I think they're better off growing up with their friends and their brothers and sisters in their own community. We know what their needs are and one of their most important needs is not to be separated out from other village kids their age as if they're misfits.'

Andy shook his head sadly, though he was also half wondering if there might not be a story in this.

'Anyway,' said Jack, 'What are things like at home? How's your little brother? What does he call himself these days – Miguel, Mikhail, Michel, Mickey?'

'Still Mikey last time I saw him.'

'Mikey! He's dodged jail then?'

'He was very, very lucky. Spirit of the times, I think.'

'You two really are very different though, aren't you?'

Andy nodded.

'Yes, I was listening to a programme on the radio the other day about disappearing regional languages. There's a language that was widely spoken somewhere in a rural area of central Europe – I was only half-listening to begin with – but it turns out that now there are only two fluent speakers of this language left in the world. And these two had some sort of argument, which developed into a feud and they haven't talked to one another for years. That's what it feels like with Mike sometimes. We share a history, an upbringing, the values passed on by our parents and yet we are largely unable to communicate in anything other than a superficial way.'

'I've never seen a pair of brothers so different. You, you're a natural sceptic, you always seem to assess the risks and decide whether they're worth it or not. Mike, sorry Mikey, he gets excited, throws caution to the wind and gets into situations he finds it difficult to get out of.'

'Expects other people to help get him out of them you mean. He never got over the '80s, never got over Thatcher. She was what he discovered on the road to Damascus.'

'Is that near Deal?'

'You know what I mean, it was his lightbulb moment. He can't see the world in any other way.'

'That boy's forgotten where he came from. What about some of the others? Billy Robson, for instance.'

'Gone away.'

'Dave Goodwin?'

'Passed away.'

'Shit. Eddie Sutcliffe?'

'Mainly pissed.'

'Kenny Roberts?'

'Permanently pissed.'

'Still, you're doing alright Andy, that's the main thing. Freelance journalist now, aren't you?'

'That's why I'm up here. I'm off to Consett tomorrow to do a piece about what life is like there fifteen years on from the closure of the steelworks.'

'There's not much left to write about now,' said Gill. 'I remember when it was a big, dirty noisy town, where just about every family was a steel worker's family. They talk about regeneration, but I can't see much of it happening there. Not even one of old Heseltine's garden festivals. So, good luck with finding something positive for your article!'

# 29

## April 1996

Andy and Mike sat in the back garden of what had, until recently, been their mother's home. Dorothy had been unable to look after herself and finally went into residential care nearby, just after Christmas. Now, with her agreement, the brothers had put the house up for sale and the estate agents' board stood in the narrow lane, at the end of the front garden.

Beyond the low garden hedge to the rear, the cornfield was still just a sea of green shoots stretching away ahead of them, but the sky was blue and the air warm.

'It's over then?'

'Yes,' Mike replied with a sigh, 'Zeta says she wants a divorce. It was always going to happen once I pleaded guilty. Banking families don't mind dirty dealing as long as it can't be traced back to them.'

'Isn't there any hope? What about marriage guidance counselling?'

'I suggested that.'

'And?'

'She agreed…'

'So there's still a chance.'

'She agreed as long I went on my own, as it's obviously all my fault.'

'Normally I'd say that's unreasonable, but possibly not in this case.'

'I know, I know. I don't have any excuse. I just got over-excited by it all, like a kid in a sweetshop.'

'So, what's going to happen now?'

'I'll tell you what I'm afraid will happen. I think they'll be able to pay their very expensive lawyers to ensure that I am left with as little as possible. They'll be on me like a packet of hyenas.'

'Pack. It's "a pack of hyenas". So, what are you going to do?'

'What can I do? I can't fight it. I have no assets. They've been seized. I need a new direction, a project to take my mind off the horrors to come.'

They gazed out over the field in silence. Mike was keen to change the subject.

'What's that bird over there?' he asked, pointing high above the poplars which marked one edge of the field.

'That's a Giant Condor,' said Andy. 'Or possibly an Emu.'

A smile spread across Mike's face and he started to laugh.

'Not a common crow then?' he said and they joined in the laughter together, in a way that they hadn't done for years. 'You know, that's the first time I've really laughed since this whole lousy business began,' Mike said, once he'd recovered himself. His demeanour became more solemn. 'Seriously Andy, you've stuck with me. No one else has. I owe you.'

Andy shook his head to disown the compliment, but added, 'You've got a second chance. Don't blow it.'

'You know that bloke you were telling me about? Perfume, or something like that.'

'John Profumo?'

'That's him. What would it take to do something like he did?'

'He worked for a charity.'

'Yes, yes, but what about doing more? You know, how about setting up a charity? What would it take to do that?'

'You need to bear in mind that with your conviction you may well be disqualified from running a charity, but even if that could be worked out it would take motivation, determination, single-mindedness...'

'I've got those.'

'Weirdly, I think you may have. So, what did you have in mind?'

'That's the trouble. I have no idea. Cats? Dogs? Old people? Donkeys?'

'If you don't have a passion and a clear direction it's not going to work.'

'I like kids. I was hoping to start a family with Zeta some time.'

Mike stared into the middle distance and there was no noise except for the distant clatter of a tractor working far away at the other end of the vast field. It was Andy who was eventually motivated to break the silence.

'Gill – you know, Jack's girlfriend – was talking to me about children with special needs. About the way in which village school closures mean they are being separated from other local children, even from their brothers and sisters.'

'Go on.' Mike seemed engaged, so Andy continued.

'There's no money and no structure for them to spend time with other children from their own communities. The danger is that they will become outsiders, alienated from their fellows. It'll almost be a sort of social cleansing. The public sector isn't going to help so perhaps a charity could.'

'Yes, yes, I get it. We could start it down here, in Kent.'

'We? I've already got a job. Not a very important one, as you've pointed out before…'

'Yeah, sorry. I didn't really mean those things. It's just I'd need help to begin with. Advice mainly. Though it would be good if you could come up with a name too. Words are your thing.'

'You've got to really want to do this you know.'

There was a sense of purpose, a new fire in Mike's eyes, glimmers of which Andy had already started to see over the previous weeks and months.

'I do, I do! The way I see it, over the course of a lifetime, people do some good things and some bad. I'm in debt. I suppose I've got an ethical overdraft. A big one. I want to do something that will help pay off what I owe.'

Andy felt himself moved by the changes that seemed to be taking place in Mike. After all, when it became clear that Dorothy could no longer look after herself it was Mike who had volunteered to research local care homes and he and Andy visited the ones he thought were best for their mother. Mike arranged for her to spend a couple of days in one of them, to see how she took to it and when it was clear that Dorothy was content, Mike managed the whole transition with dedication, enthusiasm and even sensitivity.

'I know you're working, but I've got the time, so I'll sort out the sale of the house too, if you like,' Mike had said. 'I want you to deal with the money though. I don't want anything to do with that.'

This was a Mike that Andy distantly remembered from childhood, before the spirit of the times he lived through seemed to have contaminated him. He had a natural *joie de vivre*, a desire to grasp all that life has to offer with both hands. All he had lacked, Andy reflected, was some kind of firm moral compass and perhaps that was the sort of guidance a big brother should offer. It was, he decided, his responsibility to help Mike get his life back on to some sort of sustainable path. Perhaps this would be it.

# 30

## June 1997

The trees and hedgerows were still fresh with the vivid greens they had acquired in Spring, now intensified by strong summer sunshine. In farmyards and in the corners of recently planted orchards, empty wooden boxes stencilled with the grower's name – which would eventually be used for transporting fruit – had begun to stack up, while tiny apples had started to swell along the rows of small trees. Nearby, ears of corn and barley had formed on leafy green stems in the arable fields that stretched away into the middle distance.

As he drove back through narrow country lanes to the east of Canterbury, Andy was thinking about Mike. Andy had seen stark physical changes in him. Back in the 1980s Mike had grown fleshy and comfortable, yet ill-at-ease with himself. By the time of his arrest four years earlier he had developed an unhealthy look born of self-indulgence and entitlement, his eyes dull yet somehow haunted. It was not simply that he had lost weight since then, but that his whole demeanour had changed. His eyes seemed brighter and sharper, albeit underscored by shadows which bore witness to long hours of work. His cheekbones had re-emerged, but the pale skin which stretched over them contrasted with the faint suntan of the country boy, accustomed to the outdoor life, which Andy still retained.

Andy had just been to visit his mother in her care home. It was pleasant enough, in as much as any institution where the residents await their own demise can be. Dorothy also seemed to have a new lease of life, but it was one founded largely on a make-believe world of her own devising. Many of the old gentlemen – and in truth there were not many of them when compared to the ladies – were secretly enamoured of her, at least according to her own account. One, in particular, was madly in love with her and she intended to marry him, apparently. Andy wasn't sure how far to humour Dorothy in respect of these fantasies, which seemed essentially harmless, but had the potential to spiral out of control.

His mind now drifted back again to Mike and the events of the past eighteen months. Some of them seemed barely credible to Andy.

When you are growing up with someone you see all their strengths and weaknesses at close quarters, day by day. These facets of their personality gradually bleed into your consciousness, eventually becoming firmly fixed. However, siblings who have grown apart in adulthood can each be surprised when they later discover the qualities that the other has developed independently. For all that

Andy had expressed confidence in Mike's abilities, the year or so that followed their conversation in the garden of the old family home surprised him.

It turned out that Mike could work a room and he instinctively knew which rooms were worth working too. Whether it was commercial sponsors, statutory authorities or funding organisations, he had a way of finding out about events and functions that might be useful to his project and then managed to have himself invited. He could identify the key individuals at any gathering within a few minutes and he made sure that he spoke to all of them and that they knew who he was, before he left.

Andy occasionally attended meetings with Mike and his little brother always performed impressively. He usually succeeded in getting his own way in these meetings and on the few occasions when things were going against him, Mike employed a uniquely successful strategy. He would start talking gibberish. He used terms that others in the meeting would have understood, but in a context that made no sense. Then he employed long technical sentences which, on reflection, would not have stood up to detailed analysis. He would perform *voltes-face* that left others at the meeting confused. Their fear of losing face meant Mike was rarely challenged and even if he didn't immediately get what he wanted as a result of this technique, it almost always left the door ajar.

He had even used his divorce to benefit the charity, agreeing not to fight for a settlement in return for a substantial, one-off charitable donation from the Volkovs.

He was surprisingly focused too. Given a clear set of aims Mike was able to work methodically and diligently.

He set up the charitable trust with Andy's help and between them they recruited a small core of trustees. The Chair was Angela Hardy, who had been employed in social services for a local authority and specialised in working with children with disabilities. An ex-teacher named Graham Brown was secretary of the trust and also acted as educational adviser. Mike insisted that Andy should take the role of treasurer.

'I just don't want to be anywhere near the money', he said.

Mike's *de facto* role was that of a chief operating officer, but he refused any such title and rejected even a modest salary, insisting on remaining a volunteer. He earned enough to live on by driving taxis, usually late at night and into the early hours, which helped account for the shadows under his eyes.

While he was content with the set-up, Andy reminded everyone again and again that he was a journalist, not an accountant. However, the only outcome was that he ended up writing press releases as well as keeping the books. He did as he was asked and devised a name for the charity too. As he explained to Mike they didn't want a traditional 'Society for…' prefix and it would be best to avoid the ubiquitous 'Kids', or even worse 'Kidz', that appeared in the titles of so many children's charities. After some debate they agreed it should be called *One & the Same*, because the children would all be treated as equals, they would be one and the same irrespective of ability.

As it happened, having an overview of both the finances and the trust's charitable operation gave Andy a grandstand view of its meteoric rise. By the end of its first full year more than ten thousand children of school age had benefitted from creative, sporting, social and vocational projects. From trekking in the Brecon Beacons to mixed ability sports, Mike and his ever-growing band of volunteers had success after success.

Today, as he wound through the back roads of the Garden of England, Andy found himself in reflective mood, so on a whim he decided to take a diversion and drive back to the city via the old family home. He slowed his car to a crawl, then stopped it in the single-track lane outside, in order to take everything in. All was silent and still, except for a distant high-pitched cry. He looked up and a hundred or more feet above him he could see a buzzard circling. Then another one came into view. The two called to one another as they rode the thermal currents, until one suddenly fell out of the sky, pulled into a dive and disappeared in search of its prey in the corn field opposite the house.

Although it was less than a year since the house had been sold, it was already far from being the home he had grown up in. The ragged garden hedges of flowering may and hawthorn had been supplanted by gleaming fence panels. The old front door had been replaced with something that might generously have been described as Georgian, had the Georgians had access to PVC.

Worse, from Andy's point of view, was that the old wash house had recently been demolished and a small area of flattened rubble was just visible towards the rear of the property. Andy speculated as to what the new owners might be planning there. A conservatory perhaps, or a hot tub, neither of which were unreasonable, of course, but nevertheless took the house further and further away from Andy's childhood memories. With the wash house had gone a portion of his past. He knew it was self-indulgent, but he found it hard to suppress a pang at the thought of lost childhood walks on a Sunday afternoon, splashing around in the cold waters of the shallow river below Hanging Bank Wood, the dusty school bus that trundled through the villages and the first stirrings of teenage romance.

As he drove on down into the village, Andy decided to pick up a cold drink at the store. It was a hot afternoon and the village street was sleepy and largely deserted. As he left the store, Andy stepped aside to allow a young woman, perhaps a couple of years younger than him, to enter the shop. She stopped, glanced up at him and turned away, then looked again.

'You're one of the Gibbons boys, aren't you?'

'Andy.'

'That's right. I remember your mum and dad. My mum used to do the cleaning at your house a few years back.'

'I remember.'

'I was sorry to see your mum leave the village. She were a nice lady. How is she?'

'She seems fine. I've just been to visit her at Stour Court.'

'The old folks' home?'

'That's right. She went there earlier this year – settled in quite well, I think.'

They had run out of conversation, but the young woman seemed reluctant to move on.

'There's something I really wanted to say to you, Andy…and to your brother.'

'Yes?'

'Well, I got a little boy. I got two boys actually, but the little one, Jacob, he's got problems. Asperger's. He went to school in the village last year. I was dreading it, but he done alright. That's because of his brother, of course. He goes to the school too and Jacob loves his big brother. Anyway, then they changed the rules and he had to go down to Dover, to a special school. You wouldn't believe the trouble I had with him. It's been bad. It still is, but now they both do your after-school club and go away together on the little holidays you arrange. After Easter they done camping in the New Forest. He loved it. They both loved it and the brilliant thing was they could do this stuff together.'

She looked up at him and Andy noticed the tiny wells of moisture collecting in her lower lids.

'So I just wanted to say thank you, you know, to you and your brother. It's meant the world to them. To us.'

She reached out and touched his arm, gave a shy smile, then moved inside to do her shopping. Andy walked back to his car, a little dazed by the unexpected testimonial and all that it said about the changes that had taken place in Mike and everything he had achieved.

# 31

## December 2000

Somehow or other Mike had persuaded the cathedral authorities to give the charity office space in one of the buildings within the precincts. Andy wondered if they would have been so amenable had they known that Mike had once plastered the cathedral with Tony Benn posters, some twenty years earlier.

The office was one of a number of changes that were the inevitable corollaries of the success of their enterprise. Mike had finally been persuaded to take a salary, albeit at the minimum wage and they gradually increased the professionalism of the organisation's operational base.

Now Andy wound his way up the long stone spiral staircase into the little tower room ready for a morning spent interviewing candidates for the post of part-time book-keeper. Andy had campaigned for the creation of the post and eventually he had to insist. As he pointed out again and again, the *One & the Same* charitable trust had simply grown too large for him to keep the books himself. He was prepared to continue to act as treasurer if necessary, but only if there was someone to do the number-crunching on a professional basis.

Mike was away that morning, so Andy sat on the interview panel with Angela Hardy, Chair of the Trustees and Graham Brown, the trust's Educational Adviser. Shafts of light penetrated the leaded windows and picked out motes of dust which floated around the ancient stone chamber.

They had each mentally dismissed the first two candidates, the first too young and inexperienced, the second a red faced, bottle-nosed gentleman who attempted to leave the interview room via the broom cupboard.

The next candidate, Susan Garvey, was shown in. Slim, sandy haired and in her mid-thirties, to Andy there was something instantly familiar about her. As she went to sit down they caught one another's eye and in that moment Andy knew, for all that she had changed, just who this woman was. Susan froze in the moment of sitting and coloured slightly before recovering herself.

'Er…I'm afraid I know this candidate, so I won't be able to participate in the interview,' said Andy.

'Really? Are you sure that's what you want? It's rather a small world round here, after all,' said Angela Hardy.

'Yes, I'm sorry. We used to know one another. Quite well.'

Susan nodded.

'I didn't spot it beforehand, because her surname has changed.'

'I was married,' Susan said quietly, looking down at the table in front of her.

'I'll leave you for a while and perhaps you would decide whether you want me to be here for the other interviews or not.'

'Yes, it's probably best that you just leave then, Andy,' said Angela.

Andy wound his way carefully down the narrow medieval staircase and out into the street.

*

Late that afternoon, Andy called Mike on his mobile phone.

'Hello.'

'Hi Mike. I need a word.'

'OK. How were the interviews this morning, Andy?'

'That's what I need to talk to you about.'

'Oh?'

'I've just heard who got the job.'

'Weren't you on the interview panel?'

'I had to withdraw. I had to withdraw, because one of the candidates was Susan.'

'Susan?'

'Susan Cherry. Well she's called Susan Garvey now, but when we knew her – twenty years ago – she was Susan Cherry.'

There was a long pause.

'Not sure I remember a Susan Cherry.'

'Oh yes you do. She went to your school. I went out

with her. Then…well, you and I didn't speak for eighteen months. You know why.'

'Hmm…vaguely. Still, if Angela and Graham appointed her, she must be OK. If there's a problem I'm sure you can sort it out at her induction meeting.'

'Her what?'

'You know, you carry out all the financial inductions with new staff – how to claim expenses, payroll dates, tax codes – that sort of thing.'

'Yes, but it's Susan and I don't want to…'

'If she doesn't have a notice period to work I suggest you meet her in the office on Monday morning.'

'I'm not around next week. I still have a job, something for which I'm paid. I'm a journalist, remember?'

'Oh yes. OK. I'll have the office give her a call and see if she can meet you tomorrow morning then.'

'I'm not meeting Susan in the office.'

'Alright, we'll fix it for the coffee shop in Burgate at about 11.30.'

'Wait, I'm not happy about any of this…'

'Look, I've got to go, I've got a meeting with the Dean.'

'Jesus Christ!'

'The Dean invited him too, but he couldn't make it. Talk to you later.'

Mike rang off.

*

The interior of the coffee shop had been designed entirely in brown, with complementary notes of beige, fawn and tawny. It was largely populated by what could only be described as expensively maintained middle class mothers, accompanied by a flotilla of pre-school children who were being studiously ignored as they crawled across the floors and experimented with emptying the contents of the communal sugar bowls over the tables and papering the chairs with napkins.

Andy sat stoically in a corner, with one eye on the door. He couldn't decide whether utilitarian detachment or misanthropy was his dominant mood. The mummies and their offspring were not helping alleviate the latter, in any case.

When Susan walked in she looked smart and efficient. Andy stood, shook her hand formally and offered her a seat and a cup of coffee. He adopted his most detached, business-like approach.

'So, Susan, welcome. I'm going to run through a few of the financial basics which you'll need to know when you're working for us. Let's start with the most important issue of all – payment of your salary.'

He generated a routine, mechanical smile.

'You'll be paid on the last day of every month and the money will go directly into your bank account. If we don't already have your bank details then please email them to the office so that we can get you set up on the system. Initially you will be on emergency tax, which is standard practice, until HMRC satisfy themselves that there is no outstanding tax from any previous employment. Garvey is your married name, is it not?'

There was a short silence.

'You don't have to be so formal, Andy. You know my name.'

He looked a little startled and she looked up at him, holding his gaze unflinchingly. Andy's utilitarianism crumbled.

'Yes. Yes, sorry. Standard practice, not sure how to deal with this situation…' he mumbled before tailing off.

'I don't mean to embarrass you. I just need a job. I didn't realise it would be with you two.'

There was still that faint catch in her voice, which only served to further disarm Andy.

'And I'm sorry about what happened,' she went on, 'I truly am. Nothing seemed serious back then. It was all a laugh, but now I can see how I must have hurt you, Andy. I've been hurt myself so, you know…'

'In your marriage you mean?'

'Yeah, it didn't work out so well.'

'What happened? I mean, who was he? If you don't mind me asking.'

'A squaddie from the barracks in Dover. I met him up Sutton Vale nightclub. My mum thought I was going to get pregnant and she was going to tell my dad if we didn't do the right thing. You don't know my dad.'

'I think I do.'

'Anyway, it was awful. You think it's going to be fun living with someone all the time, but it ain't. Three miserable bloody years.'

She paused and touched the side of her face, as if prompted by a hidden memory.

'It was nothing like you and me,' she said softly and Andy winced involuntarily. 'You remember that night we went to Dreamland?'

Susan smiled that shy, knowing smile and flashed a

glance at him with those irresistible eyes. Andy felt himself slipping out of his depth.

'When you held me on them Waltzers I never wanted it to stop.'

'That's exactly how I felt. I remember it so vividly. Then we went on the Ghost Train…'

'And the boating lake. Do you remember the boating lake?'

'We got soaked!'

They both found themselves laughing out loud. One or two of the mummies turned to look at them with a mixture of curiosity and irritation, ignoring the scenes of infantile carnage beneath them.

'Look, it's midday. Let's start this meeting again at the pub in the Buttermarket. We can have a drink and I'll try to welcome you with a bit more grace.'

*

Susan sat in the window seat of the pub, looking out at the Christmas shoppers hurrying through the Buttermarket, fired with Yuletide purpose and grim determination. Beside her an open fire burned steadily. Somewhere in another part of the pub she could hear an office Christmas lunch starting to get into full swing.

Andy returned with two drinks.

'There you go, a half of cider. Are you sure you don't want any rosé with it?'

Susan laughed, then looked a little embarrassed.

'I was only young Andy. I didn't know what you were talking about.'

'And I didn't know what I was doing either, but it was… Anyway, cheers!'

It took a little over ten minutes to complete Susan's induction, but they were still sitting in the pub two hours later. It was one of those December days when it never seems to get properly light. From time to time the heavens opened and the umbrellas sprouted. There was no incentive to leave the fireside and anyway they had no real idea how much time had passed.

Eventually Andy remembered he had a piece of writing he needed to do some work on that afternoon.

'I hope you feel you have all the information you need before you start work with us.'

'Oh yes, I'd forgotten about that,' she laughed.

They started walking towards the door.

'It's been lovely to see you again,' said Andy, standing at the entrance, reluctant to leave.

'What are you doing for New Year?'

'I've an invitation to a party. I don't know if I'm going to go though.'

'Do you want to come to mine?'

'Are you having a party?'

She looked him steadily in the eye and he felt her slip her hand into his.

'No.'

She held his gaze, so he understood.

'I can't think of anything I'd like more.'

# 32

## June 2001

The County Hotel bore all the hallmarks of similar establishments dotted across provincial England. It had assumed a relatively grand title, was rather over-priced and had adopted airs and graces, but it was still essentially an agglomeration of smaller buildings knocked together in order to create the largest hotel in the city. The long corridors, yellowing paint and idiosyncratic staircases and passages in many parts of the building revealed its true nature, although to a visitor from across the Atlantic the tell-tale signs may perhaps have been less apparent.

'It would be great if you could entertain him until I get back from London tomorrow,' said Mike, as they sat on a sofa in the reception area, awaiting their American visitor.

'What is he here for, exactly?'

'He's from the North Caribbean Bank.'

'What do we want with them?'

'I'll explain when I get back, but this could be big, so be nice to him, Andy. Show him the city, buy him dinner, that sort of thing.'

'OK,' said Andy doubtfully.

'Make it up as you go along. You're good at that sort of thing. You're a journalist, after all.'

Andy arched an eyebrow sceptically and they sat in silence listening to the desultory click-clack of crockery and cutlery being cleared away after lunch in the nearby dining room.

Eventually a tall, well-built figure emerged from the lift and strode confidently towards them. With his hair cut short, expensive suit and iridescent smile he looked exactly like what he was, a young American banker.

'Mike, good to see you again,' he said, grasping Mike's hand firmly.

'You too. Let me introduce you to my brother, Andrew. He's the treasurer of the trustees and signs off on all financial matters. Andy, this is Herbert Ritblatt.'

'The third.'

'Oh, yes…Herbert Ritblatt III.'

'It's a great pleasure to meet with you, Andy.'

'And you, Herbert.'

'Aw, please, call me Herb.'

'OK…Herb. May I ask what happened to the two Herbert Ritblatt prototypes?'

'Huh?'

'Well, you're the third…'

'No, No,' Herb laughed, 'That's just my Pappy and Grampy. I'm called the third so there's no confusion.'

'Well, quite. Why would there be, when you've all been given the same name, for whatever reason?'

'Look, I'm really going to have to go,' said Mike. 'I have a train to catch.'

'Sure thing, Mike,' said Herb, 'we'll have a powwow tomorrow, yeah?'

'Of course. I'll look forward to it.'

Mike departed hastily.

'So, what's the programme, Andy?'

'Ah...' Andy was taken by surprise. There was no programme. 'Well, if you're interested in sightseeing there's the old city wall and the Westgate Tower.'

'An old wall.'

'Then there are the various museums.'

Herb looked unimpressed.

'And the cathedral, of course, the seat of the Church of England, which dates from the 11th century.'

'Lot of very old stuff here,' said Herb without enthusiasm.

'What do you like doing at home?' asked Andy in desperation.

'I guess I spend a lot of time watching MLB. That's what my wife would say anyway!'

'MLB?'

'Major League Baseball. I don't miss a Marlins game when I'm in town.'

'Marlins?'

'Miami Marlins.'

'There's not really much baseball played in England, beyond the occasional game of rounders in the park.'

'Rounders?'

'It doesn't matter. I think Kent might be playing today, up at the cricket ground, but cricket is rather an arcane game, so I'm not sure if…'

'I don't understand any of that, but it's sport, right? Let's give it a go. Beats looking at old stuff any day.'

It was a perfect afternoon for it. The St Lawrence ground was bathed in sunshine and a few light cumulus glided overhead. There was real heat in the air, but it was tempered by a steady, gentle breeze. Andy and Herb made their way into the ground just in time for the afternoon session. For some reason Herb tried to tip the startled gateman with a dollar bill as they made their way in. They found seats in the small stand next to the pavilion, in the company of a dozen or so old gentlemen wearing jackets and ties and clutching copies of the *Daily Telegraph*. Some of them were accompanied by wives who bore a long-suffering look.

Herb looked around, taking it all in and he was staring at something particularly intently, yet uncomprehendingly.

'What's that?'

'It's the scoreboard.'

'What's all that math mean?'

'It means that Kent have scored 97 runs, but two of their batsmen are out.'

'Is that good?'

'It's too early to tell.'

'Too early! How long have these guys been playing?'

'A couple of hours.'

'A couple of hours and you don't even know who's winning! What time does it finish?'

'Tonight it finishes at 6.30, but it's a four day game.'

'Four days? Jeez! Don't you guys get bored?'

The players had returned to the pitch and the first over was bowled. It was a maiden.

'So what just happened?' asked Herb, loud enough that some of the old gentlemen awoke from their afternoon naps and turned to look at him.

'It was a maiden over. No runs, no wickets.'

'Huh!'

So it continued, with Herb's eyebrows knitted in concentration. The Kent third wicket partnership prodded and pushed, grinding the score on to 122. After an hour or so their opponents decided to try bowling their leg spinner from the pavilion end. The first ball was duly prodded gently back down the wicket. As the second was delivered, the batsman advanced from his crease and clubbed the ball straight down the ground. It sailed over the boundary and clattered into the top tier of the stand, a couple of rows in front of them.

Herb was on his feet whooping.

'Woohoo! Way to go!' he yelled before Andy grabbed him by the arm and gently but firmly pulled him back into his seat. The old gentlemen had broken into a smattering of applause, little louder than the sound of a crisp packet being gently crumpled.

By the end of the day, Herb had decided that, while it was nothing like as good as MLB, he 'kinda liked' cricket. The glasses of chilled white Sauvignon that Andy brought him from time to time probably helped his appreciation of the game. What perplexed him though was the large lime tree which grew just inside one of the boundary ropes.

'What's it doing there? I mean, why don't they just take it out?'

'It's been there for more than 150 years. The cricket ground was built around it.'

'You build a sports field with a big tree in it. Makes no sense to me.' He shook his head, but Andy suspected that Herb was developing a sneaking regard for the anachronistic ways of the English.

The shadows lengthened and play drew to a close. The players left the field to a little polite applause from those left in the ground.

'So, shall we get something to eat?' asked Andy.

'I'm hungry as a hog.'

'Well, what do you want?'

'Is British food really as bad as they say?'

'No, restaurants in this country have been improving rapidly. It's certainly a lot better than when I was a boy.'

'OK, let's go get some British food.'

'Hmm. Most of the best restaurants have French or Italian or Oriental influences, but there is a little place by the river which specialises in pies. It's not bad.'

A couple of steak and kidney pies and a bottle of red wine later they considered themselves fed and now Herb wanted to go to a typical English pub.

'OK, if you're sure.'

'Sure I'm sure,' said Herb, leaving a ten dollar bill as a tip.

As they left, a young man who was about to enter the restaurant held the door open for them and Herb surprised him by pressing a dollar bill into his hand as he passed.

'He wasn't the doorman you know,' said Andy as they walked along the high street.

'No kidding?'

'No kidding.'

Herb suddenly halted and gripped Andy's arm.

'Let's go in here. Look – The Cricketers. Seems kind of appropriate.'

They pushed their way in to the small front bar.

'So what do I drink in an English pub?'

'Beer. Real ale.'

'OK, I'll have a bottle of that.'

'No, it rarely comes in bottles. It's drawn up from a cask in the cellar by these handpumps.'

The girl behind the bar, who had a broad smile and a gap between her front teeth, pulled two pints.

Andy and Herb found a couple of empty seats at the back of the bar. They walked over to them with their pints and noticed the girl following them. When she arrived at their table she held up a damp, limp five dollar bill.

'You left this on the bar.'

'There's no need to tip every time you're served a drink in a pub,' said Andy to Herb with a little exasperation.

'Americans are known for being good tippers. I got a reputation to maintain.'

They picked up their pints, clinked glasses and drank. Herb stopped in mid-sip and peered at Andy suspiciously.

'Is this beer?'

'It is. It may take a little getting used to, but it's a fine pint here.'

Herb looked unconvinced and Andy felt a little uncomfortable.

'OK, I'll tell you what. Let's have whisky chasers. That may introduce you to the beer via a more palatable route.'

'Bourbon or Rye?'

'Scotch.'

As Andy went back to the bar Herb shouted, 'Better make those Scotches big ones Andy.'

Andy rolled his eyes and the girl with the diastema smiled.

'I think he's well on his way already,' said Andy.

'I see what you mean. I've got to change the optic, so I'll bring them over to you.'

'He'll only give you more damp dollar bills.'

Andy told Herb he was going to the Gents, which he had to explain was the English equivalent of the American 'bathroom'. When he returned a few minutes later, things certainly seemed to have livened up in the bar and there almost seemed to be a party atmosphere. Herb and his drinks were missing, but Andy followed the noise and located him sitting at the centre of a large group of people by the window.

'Hey, Andy, come on over,' shouted Herb above the hubbub. 'I want you to meet these people. Not only are they good Americans, but they're from Chippewa Falls. Some coincidence, huh? We grew up almost next door neighbours.'

The other Americans agreed noisily.

'I thought you were from Miami.'

'That's where I live now, but I grew up in Milwaukee. Can you believe that? It's just three hundred miles from Chippewa Falls.'

'No – maybe two fifty at most,' protested one of the other Americans.

'Well, what an extraordinary coincidence,' said Andy drily.

'Get your drinks and come sit with us, Andy.'

Andy did as he was asked and the evening proceeded raucously. Herb introduced the other Americans to Scotch chased down with a real ale and *The Cricketers* rang to the sound of trans-Atlantic laughter.

'So where are you gonna go after England, Herb?' asked one of his new friends.

'I wanna visit some of the big cities in this part of Yurp: Paris, Berlin, Belgium…'

'Belgium isn't really a city, Herb,' said Andy.

'No?'

'No, it's more of a country.'

The Americans laughed happily at Herb and Herb laughed along.

Eventually the Chippewa Falls party had to return to their hotel and departed with various whoops and cheers. It was clear that Herb, who had been drinking for most of the afternoon and evening, had probably had enough.

'Aw, I've had a great day, Andy. A great day.'

'I'm really pleased. I've enjoyed it too, but don't you think we should be getting you back to the County Hotel if you're going to be fresh for your meeting with Mike tomorrow?'

Herb fell uncharacteristically silent and thoughtful. He leaned forward until he could breathe alcohol fumes over Andy.

'Andy. Andy, Andy, Andy, Andy…'

'Yes.'

'I like you. Andy, you wanna tell your little brother…' Herb supressed a belch, '…you wanna tell your little brother to take care.'

Andy had no idea what he was talking about and just raised an inquisitive eyebrow.

'I like you and I don't want to see you guys in over your heads.'

Something in Herb suddenly seemed to snap back in to place and he shouted, 'OK. Let's go. Back to the County Hotel!'

# 33

## September 2003

Andy dropped a pile of manila files onto Mike's desk in his office in the cathedral precincts. In response, motes of dust floated up through the shafts of light pouring in through the narrow window of the tower room.

'Those are the returns for the last two quarters, Mike. I haven't checked them, because I haven't had time, but Susan knows what she's doing.'

'That's fine. She has all of this in her computer files. She can email it to me. She's great, really good at her job.'

'She is. I guess once you know your way around the balance sheets it's just like riding a bike.'

'I remember when I was learning to ride a bike,' Mike said with a smile.

'Don't we all? You'd pedal that little bike of yours as fast as you could along the concrete slabs of the farm track opposite the house.'

'It was great.'

'Except that you didn't really know how to steer other than in a straight line and it took you ages to work out how to use the brakes. At the point you reached the hedgerow at the end of the track you'd just crash, every single time. You were covered in grazes, bruises and mud all the while you were learning.'

'I think I was what these days we have to call "an experiential learner" Andy.'

'You were a kamikaze maniac. I think Mum was afraid you'd break your neck.'

'I didn't realise you'd noticed. I thought you were always too busy scanning the skies for red crates.'

'Kites. It's red kites.'

Mike laughed. He was in reflective, yet effusive mood and it showed in every toothy smile.

'You were a good brother to me Andy, but we sort of went our own ways later on.'

'I know. You always seemed to be searching for the holy grail, or the philosophers' stone or whatever. You thought there was one simple answer to everything in life and you just needed to find it.'

'Oh yeah, I remember all those self-help books I read to try and find out what it was.'

'Self-help books to which you helped yourself from the library, because your library ticket was out of date,' replied Andy.

'There was one I really liked: *Feed Your Inner Hero – your complete guide to getting what you want when you want it!*'

'You followed every fad. Remember when you had that designer stubble?'

'I looked like George Michael. Actually no, more like Don Johnson from *Miami Vice*.'

'You just looked like you needed a shave.'

They both laughed.

'And all those get rich quick schemes you had. The defroster, for example,' said Andy.

'I remember you used to wind me up though. What was it you reckoned would sell well – novelty deodorants?'

'People love the smell of bacon cooking. Why not try it as a deodorant?'

'I was almost tempted by the comedy bereavement cards idea,' said Mike, then changed tack. 'You know, going back to talking about Susan again, I was thinking just the other day, it's so great that you two are back together again. After such a long time and everything.'

'Yeah, it's good. Thanks.'

'How long is it now? Three years?'

'Yes. Maybe we should leave that subject. You know, given the history.'

'Sure, sure. Still, everything's going pretty well for you at the moment – personally and professionally, I mean. I'm glad. You deserve it.'

'Well, you know, there's always a serpent in paradise… but thanks.'

'Are you finding it difficult to fit everything in? What with pitching for magazine and newspaper jobs, writing and everything, as well as the work you're doing here. You need to make time to see Susan too.'

'It can be a little difficult. I wish I had more time, certainly.'

'That's what I've thought, so I want to arrange for some

of the work that currently falls to you to be signed off by Susan. OK with you?'

'Which work?'

'Just some of the transfers between accounts. We need to maintain our reserves so we must make sure we're getting the best returns on our deposits. It's an important income stream for a small charity like us.'

'I know. Which deposits do you mean?'

'Just one or two of them, like – say – the North Caribbean Bank account. It should save you quite a bit of time.'

The phone on the desk rang and Mike picked it up.

'Yes. This is Michael Gibbons speaking. OK, that's great, I'll be there to view the property at three o'clock,' he said before replacing the receiver.

'Since when did anyone call you Michael, apart from Mum?'

'I just think it gives me a little more gravitas. People realise I'm a force to be reckoned with.'

Mike smiled, but Andy looked sceptical.

'So what was the property you were talking about, Mike?'

'A little house down near the river. I want to buy a place of my own. I mean renting is better than squatting at your place like I did in the early days, but it's time I had somewhere of my own.'

'How's that going to work? You're on the minimum wage.'

'Oh, you know, I've saved quite a bit from when I used to drive taxis at all hours. I have enough for a deposit shall we say. You can't rest on your laurels, you have to move forward in this life.'

'I don't think we have any alternative. Time takes care of that, whether we like it or not.'

'Maybe. Either way, I'm ready for the next step.'

*

Out in the street loose squadrons of schoolchildren were making their way to or from the cathedral. The lure of St Thomas à Becket had brought large numbers of them across the channel. Once their teachers were out of sight many chose to squirt each other with foam or 'Silly String', turning the streets into a sort of juvenile Saturnalia, of which the sainted Thomas would have been unlikely to approve.

In the midst of all this Andy spotted a face he knew. He made straight for her.

'Auntie Sheila!'

'Hello Andy, I knew you worked round here, but I didn't expect to see you.'

'Shouldn't you be behind the bar in the club? What are you doing in the city?'

'Hospital appointment. It's my hip again. I don't like coming up here. Even after all these years I'm not sure we're really welcome.'

'Don't be silly. Times have changed. It's not like that any more.'

'I'm not so sure. What are you up to then, Andy?'

'I've just been with Mike in the charity office, at the other end of Burgate.'

Sheila said nothing, scrutinising Andy carefully for a moment.

'You take care with him. You know what I mean.'

'Mike? He's a changed man, Auntie Sheila, believe me.'

'That's all I'm saying. Look after your own interests first. You're too nice Andy. Don't get taken advantage of.'

'What do you mean?'

'Look, I've got to go love. My appointment's in fifteen minutes and I've got to walk up that hill. Just take care.'

And with that she was gone.

# 34

## July 2004

There is a sense of bathos, of all-encompassing anti-climax, about a theme park after a thunderstorm. It was the end of the day and the air had cooled a little after the heat and humidity of the afternoon. Now great pools of water lay on the tarmac walkways following the earlier deluge. The rides had stopped and a few stragglers wandered aimlessly around the site.

Most importantly, Andy and Susan had packed the last children onto the *One & the Same* coach. Staff and volunteer holidays meant the charity was short-staffed, so Susan had been drafted in from the office to help manage the outing. Andy had no immediate deadlines to meet, so he had agreed when Mike asked him to help out too. Privately he had relished the idea of a day out with Susan, irrespective of the circumstances. They had been together again for three years now, but they still lived apart, except at weekends.

Andy might have been inclined to change that situation and suggest that they move in together, but Susan remained elusive, unquantifiable and seemed content to leave things as they were. If the subject ever came up she would simply say, 'What we got is great Andy. Why change it?' Andy had no answer to that, just a nagging feeling that at some point things would have to change. For the time being, however, they both still seemed to have retained the kind of mutual attraction which can be enhanced by periods of time apart.

'Shall we get a coffee or something?'

It had been a long day, counting children on and off the roller-coaster rides, trying to stop some of the boys jumping into the water at the end of the log flume and keeping everyone together when there were temptations and attractions at every turn. It was like herding cats.

'OK, there's a McDonald's just down there.'

'Really? I mean, will the coffee be OK?'

'This is an adventure theme park Andy, not a specialist coffee shop. If you're looking for one of them cappuccino macchiato things you're going to be disappointed wherever we go.'

'I know. I always think it's funny that in those places the coffee and the portions are all in Italian, but if I try speaking to the staff in a little bit of basic Italian they haven't a clue what I'm talking about.'

'You won't have any problem in Maccy D's. It's just called coffee there. Large or small.'

The interior was gloomy in spite of the garish décor and the smell of burger and chips hung in the air. Desultory diners gazed out of the windows in the direction of what might have been their last rides of the day.

Susan's mobile phone, provided by the charity, pinged. She looked at her text message, raised her eyebrows and typed her reply. She looked up at Andy.

'It's Mike. He's in the main car park.'

'Here?'

'Yes. He's on his way into London and he wanted to check everything went OK today. I told him it was fine, but I said we were finished so we'd go out and talk to him since he's here.'

'Gives me an excuse not to finish this coffee.'

'What are you like? There's nothing wrong with it!'

'I bet my brother wouldn't drink it. Tell me Susan, you see him on a daily basis, has my brother changed at all in the last couple of years, do you think?'

'Changed?'

'You know, when he started *One & the Same* he was a man transformed. He'd become quieter, more focused, determined to do the right thing. He worked day and night you know. He'd be setting up the charity until evening and then afterwards he'd do a shift on the taxis. In the last couple of years something seems to have changed. I can't quite put my finger on it.'

'He's pretty much like I always knew him. Then I didn't ever know him as well as I know you.' She smiled at him.

They walked back to the main gate hand in hand. There, Mike greeted them with a big smile.

'Everything OK today, Andy?'

'Yes fine, thanks. We're both pretty dead on our feet, but the kids had a great time.'

'I know. The abilities were really mixed in that group you had today, so it was bound to be hard work.'

'Yeah, but they were lovely. A lot of those who could were helping out those who found it more difficult. Sweet kids, bless them,' said Susan.

'Where are you off to, Mike?' Andy wondered.

'Kids Charity of the Year awards in London. I'm hoping we might pick something up.'

'Are you driving back tonight?'

'No. I'm staying over at the Royal Garden.'

'Oh…well…very nice for you.' Andy was a little taken aback.

'Anyway, I've got to dash. I don't want to be late. Thanks to you both for everything you've done today.' He flashed a smile, turned on his heel and walked across the car park.

Andy watched him go, weaving between the remaining cars, before stopping beside a bright blue Porsche Boxster and climbing in. Andy turned to look at Susan, but she didn't seem to have registered what had just happened.

# 35

## November 2007

It was already dark and the cobbled streets around the cathedral glistened in the rain as Andy walked home. His mobile phone rang and he ducked into a shop doorway to answer it.

'Hey Andy, it's Herb. Herb Ritblatt,' he added, unnecessarily.

'Hello Herb. It's been a while. How are you?'

'I'm good, I'm good. How are things with you in Canterbury? How's the cricket?'

'Oh, it's the close season now, but Kent had another indifferent summer. Nothing much changes.'

'Why am I not surprised! Listen Andy, I know I normally talk with Mike, but well you and me…we got a bond. I told you, I like you.'

'Thank you.'

'So I wanna give you a heads up here fella.'

'Er…OK.'

'You know the three things this great nation was founded on?'

'You mean America?'

'Money, family and God. Well things have changed. We tried to keep the myth of the great American family going as long as we could, but we all know that it's all washed-up. Then there's God. He kinda gave the game away about his own non-existence, at least that's the way most folk figure it. So that just leaves money, it's all we got.'

'So?'

'So, the shit's about to hit the fan.'

Andy paused. This wasn't what he was expecting. He didn't deal with the North Caribbean Bank under normal circumstances and Herb was making no sense.

'What do you mean, Herb?'

'I mean the money tree is about to stop producing.'

'You're talking in riddles. Tell me exactly what you mean.'

'I'll give it to you straight, Andy. A whole heap of the finance deals are about to come crashing down.'

'What deals?'

'You know the money we've been investing for your charity, right?'

'Well yes, of course, it's there in the accounts, but these are relatively modest sums, right?'

'Wrong. At least, they may be modest when they arrive with us, but once we've finished investing they're big, real big, at least on paper.'

'I'm the treasurer, I know the sums involved. I know what's in the bank.'

Herb was silent for a moment.

'You know about the accounts in the Cayman Islands, right?'

'No! What accounts are those?'

'Alright, then I guess you need to know. We take your money, we invest, we send most of the profit – and we're talking big bucks – to banks in the Cayman Islands. No tax, no questions asked.'

'Jesus Christ! I didn't know this. Look, Herb, exactly how are you managing to get such big financial returns?'

'That's the point Andy. It's all sub-prime and short selling and that's about to come to an end, big time. We can't run those numbers any more.'

'I'm sorry, I didn't understand any of your last sentence at all.'

'You want me to level with you, Andy? It was money for nothing. Everyone knew it couldn't last, but we rode that train as far as we could…'

'Is it all legitimate, you know, legal?'

Andy could hear other voices at Herb's end.

'Sorry Andy, gotta go. There's a toga party round the pool here this evening. Look after yourself Andy and say "hi" to Mike.'

The phone went dead and left Andy staring through the rain at the orange glow of the street lamps.

# 36

## December 2007

'I want to know what Herb meant.'

Andy stood amidst the swags and drapes of Mike's living room, beside a mock-Regency chair. Under other circumstances he might have wondered why his brother's taste in interior design seemed stuck in a previous decade. Beyond the room's French windows, at the end of Mike's garden, the grey green River Stour gently wound its way through the city, but Andy's mind was elsewhere.

'I'm really worried Mike. "Big bucks" he said. In accounts I didn't even know existed. In the Cayman Islands, for God's sake!'

Andy continued in this vein for some time and Mike let the storm blow itself out. A seagull landed in the little garden, managed a couple of routine pecks at the grass and took flight again. From somewhere along the river there was a distant quacking of ducks.

'Sit down, Andy.'

'I'm fine standing.'

'Look, I know Herb.'

'I know Herb too and he frightened me. I've tried to call him back several times, but it just goes straight to voicemail.'

'We both know Herb, though I know him a little better than you do. He has a sense of humour doesn't he?'

'So?'

'We both know Herb likes a joke. What was it he said that he had to go off to, at the end of your call?'

'A toga party.'

Mike smiled and shook his head.

'Good old Herb, he never changes.'

'So what about this account in the Cayman Islands?'

'There isn't one. It was a joke. Herb was winding you up. He does the same to me sometimes.'

'Really? It didn't sound very funny.' Andy was unsure of his ground.

'He's an American! They have a different style of humour. They love a practical joke.'

'What was meant to be the hilarious outcome of this one then?'

'This! You were meant to be wound up and then to come and wind me up too. It hasn't worked – at least, not entirely.'

He sat down on the sofa and Andy slowly followed his lead, glancing out towards a tiny boat in which a couple of very cold and miserable tourists were being rowed slowly along the river.

'Andy, you've seen it all with your own eyes. I've turned

my life around, I've built this charity up from nothing. We're award winners, TV regulars, the go-to charity for kids, we're the benchmark for others. I haven't done that on my own, I've needed Angela and Graham and Susan and everyone else, but most of all, I've relied on you – on my brother. You know what's happened and how it happened, you know what I've put into this.

'I realise I made mistakes earlier in my life, but I couldn't seem to find the right niche. I never wanted to follow the herd, you see. I didn't have your education, but I knew I didn't want a menial nine to five job, a wife who comes to despise me and a couple of children I only see at weekends.

'You've seen it all yourself. These people grind it day in, day out and all for what? Two weeks holiday each year, somewhere affordable in the sun and a miserable affair with the girl from HR who lives with her mother and has self-esteem issues. Once the wife has cleared off with the kids and most of the money then these guys turn to booze or gambling or whatever else to console themselves.

'They're losers Andy and I didn't want to be like that. I know I took the wrong path – lots of wrong paths – but I found the right one eventually. With your help I found the right one. I'm not going to jeopardise all that. Herb's just a joker…an American joker.'

Andy still looked doubtful, troubled, though somewhat less so than he had been earlier.

'You're saying there are no hidden funds, no bank accounts in the Cayman Islands?'

'You know the charity doesn't have anything like that, Andy. You'd be the first to know if we did. You're the treasurer after all.'

They made their way into the hall, where the window blind beside the front door appeared, to Andy's eye, to be made from a pair of old silk bloomers. Beneath it there was a pair of stiletto-heeled patent leather ankle boots.

'Got yourself a new hobby, Mike?'

Mike laughed.

'They're not my size. I enjoy a little female company from time to time though. I can't always be working.'

There was a pause and they looked one another in the eye.

'Look…you are being straight about everything aren't you? Herb was just joking wasn't he?'

Mike smiled broadly.

'You know me, Andy, I'm a changed man. Anyway, you're my brother. I wouldn't betray your trust.'

# 37

## February 2008

There was a sullen winter light behind the bedroom curtains. Andy rolled out of bed and drew them back to reveal a miserable grey sky, the window panes flecked with rain. He screwed up his face in displeasure.

'The weather forecast said it was going to be a crisp, sunny winter morning.'

Susan laughed from beneath the sheets.

'Never trust a weather forecaster,' she said.

'It looks like a walk on Walmer beach is out of the question. At least it is for me.'

'Ahh,' she said, in mock sympathy, 'are you going to miss your birdwatching?'

'I'm not a bird watcher! I just happen to know the difference between a magpie and a crow.'

'No wonder your brother calls you "nature boy".'

'He doesn't. At least he hasn't done for a long time. So what shall we do then?'

'Let's start with you making me a cup of tea. Then we can decide after that.'

He smiled, kissed her and went into the kitchen to put the kettle on.

Steam was rising and the kettle was beginning to bubble when the Sunday newspapers were pushed noisily through the letterbox. Andy returned with tea and the papers.

'Which bit do you want?'

'Oh, you know…give me the bit with the celebs and the gossip!'

Andy shook his head sadly and climbed back into bed.

'OK, if you really want all that formulaic emoting.'

'What do you mean?'

'I mean that all of this stuff,' he waved the magazine, 'is unnatural, it's learned behaviour, it's playing to the crowd…'

'Learned from where?'

'TV programmes mostly, I guess. They learn their emotional responses from soap operas and reality shows.'

'They don't.'

'They do. They can't help it. It's a bit like what they say about sexual responses becoming conditioned by the amount of internet pornography being consumed nowadays…'

'Well you'd know,' she laughed and poked him in the ribs, hard.

Andy yelped. 'That's not fair! It's not true either. I suppose we could go round to see if Mike's in and take him out to lunch later. Have you been to his new house yet?'

'Yes, maybe once or twice.'

'I was round there the other day.'

'Oh yes.'

'In his hall there were a pair of stiletto boots best suited to a fetish film.'

'Oh, really.' Susan appeared uninterested.

'They weren't his size, so how do you think they got there?'

Andy didn't have time to pursue this idea, because his mobile phone on the bedside table began to ring. Andy looked at his watch, frowned and answered it.

'Hello.'

'Hi! Is that...' There was a brief pause. 'Andrew Gibbons?'

'Yes.'

'This is Steve from RNJ. How are you today sir?' This did not sound like any Steve that Andy had ever spoken to and English was clearly not his first language. Andy sighed.

'What are you selling?'

'I'm not selling anything, sir,' said Steve sounding a little hurt.

'Then why are you calling me at eight o'clock on a Sunday morning?'

There was a short pause, as if Steve was adjusting to the idea that it might be 8am on a Sunday.

'This isn't selling Andrew, we're undertaking a brand awareness-broadening exercise. We are the leading suppliers of...'

Andy terminated the call, having wearied of Steve not selling him anything.

'Friend of yours?' asked Susan.

Andy just made an exasperated noise in response. At that moment the front doorbell rang and Andy buried his head under the cover. The caller rang the bell again.

'Who's that calling at this time on a Sunday morning, Andy?'

'Surprisingly, I won't know until I've opened the door. That's the traditional way of finding out.'

Andy climbed out of bed and began to put on a pair of trousers, then shuffled along to the front door in his slippers and opened it, to reveal two men.

'Andrew Gibbons?'

'Yes.'

'We're police officers. May we come in?'

The officers showed Andy their warrant cards and stepped into the hallway.

There were specks of rain on the shoulders of the first policeman's fawn coloured gaberdine.

'My name is Inspector James Curtly, this is Sergeant Green. Andrew Kenneth Gibbons...'

Andy's head started to swim. This wasn't real, it was like a scene from a film. Yet it was happening. He felt distant, as if he was looking at it dispassionately, as if he was part of an audience.

'...I am arresting you on suspicion of Conspiracy to Defraud, Fraudulent Misrepresentation, Misappropriation of Financial Assets and the Preparation of Fraudulent Financial Statements. You do not have to say anything, but it may harm your defence if you do not mention when questioned something which you later rely on in court. Anything you do say may be given in evidence.'

# Epilogue

## May 2010

Andy looked pale and grey in his prison clothes, Mike thought. The reduced state in which he found his brother reminded him what a shrewd call it had been to plead guilty back in '95. He shivered at the thought of what a prison sentence would have done to him.

Mike sat down in the chair opposite, but Andy did not look pleased to see him.

'Oh, it's you,' was all he said.

'Who were you expecting?'

'It doesn't matter. You've got a nerve to keep coming here. There's no point in it you know.'

It wasn't a good start. Perhaps, Mike thought, Andy needed to be reminded that there was a world beyond the prison walls. He needed to be prompted to remember that there would still be a life full of opportunities on the outside when he came out.

'You're wrong there, big brother, there's every point.'

'Like?'

'If you don't stay positive you're going to miss out.'

Andy gave a hollow laugh. 'On what?'

'Well…opportunities. The point is that there's nothing that isn't a potentially valuable commodity these days. Everything has a price, even if it's not a monetary one. We all have to trade with each other, all the time.'

'Don't be ridiculous.'

Mike was undeterred.

'I'll give you an example. The big one – love! It's about finer feelings, exists on a higher plane, right? Wrong. We're trading the whole time. When someone says they love you, even just casually – like when they sign off a phone call – you have a choice about whether to meet their stated valuation of the relationship or not.'

'You make it sound like a card game. I see your "love you" and raise you a "you are my soul mate".'

'Yeah, something like that. You're getting the idea.'

'I hate to dampen your enthusiasm, Mike, but those are the least of my problems right now. I'm locked up when it's you who should be inside.'

'Calm down Andy. That's just not fair. Look, do you know when you are due for – you know – release?'

'If my appeal fails, you mean?'

'Well, yes. If it does.'

'2016. June 24th 2016. I can only hope that life in this country will have started to make a bit more sense by then.'

There was a long pause while Mike took this in. He seemed distracted and kept looking at his watch.

'Andy this is only a flying visit, I'm going to have to go soon.'

'Why?'

'There's someone waiting in the car for me, out in the car park.'

'Who?'

'It doesn't matter, but she's been there over an hour.'

'What's her name?'

Mike remained silent and looked evasive, but Andy was starting to work things out for himself.

If he had looked pale and washed out when Mike arrived, he looked even greyer now.

'I've not had a visit, or a letter in weeks. It's Susan in the car outside, isn't it?'

'It doesn't matter who it is.'

'It bloody does!'

'Be reasonable Andy, I don't have to ask you for permission. You're in here…'

'Thanks to you.'

'You know that's not true. Anyway, the point is that you're in here and well…we're on the outside. So, you know, that's just the way life is. I've told you. We all have to take our opportunities.'

'You bastard!'